GOOD-BYE STACEY, GOOD-BYE

GOOD-BYE STACEY, GOOD-BYE

Ann M. Martin

AN
APPLE
PAPERBACK

SCHOLASTIC INC.
New York Toronto London Auckland Sydney

With Love to Peanut Butter
From Jelly

Cover art by Hodges Soileau

ISBN 0-590-25168-6

12 11 10 9 8 7 6 5 4 3 2 1   12   5 6 7 8 9/9 0/0

Printed in the U.S.A.   40

CHAPTER 1

I was daydreaming.

In my fantasy, I had walked into Candy Land. Not the little kids' game, but a real land where everything was made of candy. You know, peppermint-stick lampposts and rivers of chocolate and fields of green icing. I stopped and sampled everything I saw — a lick of peppermint, a slurp of chocolate, a mouthful of icing.

I have to tell you, even *I* thought the fantasy was pretty lame, but the thing is, I've got diabetes, which means I have to limit the amount of sweets I eat — which means no candy or sugary junk food. I've had diabetes for almost two years now. That's close to twenty-four months without white chocolate and root beer barrels and Twinkies and Ring Dings and Yodels. I try to pretend that this doesn't matter, but the truth is — sometimes I'd kill for a Tootsie Pop.

So you can see why I was dreaming about Candy Land.

It was unfortunate though, that I was dreaming during math class. When my teacher called on me, I answered, "Huh?" Now, ordinarily, I'm a pretty good student, especially in math, so Mr. Zizmore looked confused. I was saved by the bell, though, and gratefully escaped into the hallway. School was over for the day, and I had a busy afternoon ahead of me.

First I was going to baby-sit for one of the greatest little kids in the world. Then I was going to go to a meeting of the Baby-sitters Club. The Baby-sitters Club was the reason I had the job in the first place. The club is really a sitting business that I run with four of my friends.

"Stacey! Stacey!" someone called.

I turned around, trying to open my locker at the same time. "Oh, hi, Claud!" I replied.

Claudia Kishi is my best friend here in Stoneybrook, Connecticut. (I have another best friend, Laine Cummings, in New York City, which is where I used to live.) Claud came running toward me, her black hair flying.

"What's up?" I asked her.

"You will never guess what I just heard."

"What?" I pulled my French book and a pair

of dirty gym socks out of my locker and stuffed them into my knapsack.

"Are you in a hurry?" asked Claudia.

"Yeah. I'm sitting for Charlotte Johanssen today. I'm supposed to be at her house by three. . . . What did you hear?"

"That Howie Johnson asked Dorianne Wallingford to go to the library with him this afternoon."

I frowned. Howie wasn't exactly my boyfriend. In fact, he wasn't my boyfriend at all. But he had taken me to the last few school dances. So why was he asking Dori to study with him?

"Maybe they're doing a group project together or something," I suggested. But I was far more hurt than I let on, even though there was no reason to feel that way.

"Yeah. That must be it." Claudia slipped her arm comfortingly across my shoulders. "Come on. I'll walk you to Charlotte's. And then I'll see you at the club meeting later."

Claudia left me at the Johanssens' driveway. We had talked about Howie all the way from Stoneybrook Middle School to Charlotte's house.

We had decided that Howie was a jerk.

When I rang the Johanssens' bell, Charlotte met me at the door, bouncy and happy as usual. She's my favorite kid and I'm her favorite sitter.

"Hi!" she cried. "Hi, Stacey! Guess what — I got invited to a sleepover party! It's at Vanessa Pike's and we're going to go to the *movies* first. Four of us. Me and Vanessa and Suki and Merry."

Charlotte stopped chattering only long enough to let her mother give me instructions for the afternoon. As soon as Dr. Johanssen left, Charlotte began talking again. Sometimes I just couldn't get over how she had changed since I first baby-sat for her. That was a year ago, when she was seven. She was quiet then, and sad, and had no friends her age. Now she's happy and friendly and has a new best girl-friend each week. Her mother says half the change is due to the fact that Charlotte wasn't being challenged enough at school and needed to skip a grade (which she did) — and the other half is due to *me!* According to Dr. Johanssen, I helped Charlotte learn a lot about herself and about getting along with kids. That makes me feel terrific. Also, it's kind of nice to be somebody's favorite person. (But it's scary, too.)

When I left Charlotte's, it was almost 5:30, so I ran straight to Claudia's house. The meetings of the Baby-sitters Club are held in Claudia's bedroom since she has her own phone *and* her own phone number. Also for this reason, Claudia is the vice-president of the club.

The president is Kristy Thomas. Kristy was the one who had the original idea to start a baby-sitting club. (Kristy is full of ideas.) The sign of a good businessperson, my dad always says, is the ability to recognize a problem and find a way to solve it (a money-making way to solve it, that is). And that's exactly what Kristy did a year ago. She saw what a hard time her mother was having trying to find a sitter for her little brother, David Michael. Her mom had to make one call after another, looking for someone who was free. What Kristy thought was, Wouldn't it be great if her mom could find a sitter with just one phone call? And now our club provides that service. When somebody calls Claudia's number on a Monday, Wednesday, or Friday afternoon between 5:30 and 6:00, they reach Claudia (of course), Kristy, Mary Anne Spier, Dawn Schafer, and me, Stacey McGill.

We are the members of the Baby-sitters Club.

As I've said, Kristy is the president and Claudia is the vice-president. The secretary is Mary Anne. Her job is to schedule baby-sitting appointments and to keep track of the stuff in our club record book. The record book is where we write down the names and addresses of our clients, important club information, and our sitting jobs.

It's also where we keep track of the money we earn, but that's my job. I'm the treasurer. I'm responsible for collecting our club dues, too. Each week, the five of us put some money into our treasury. The money pays for Kristy's big brother Charlie to drive her to and from meetings, since she moved out of the neighborhood last summer, and it buys treats for ourselves (like pizzas), as well as club supplies.

Dawn Schafer is our alternate officer. Her job is to take over the duties of any other club member who can't come to a meeting for some reason. Let me tell you, she got her fill of being vice-president recently when Claudia missed meeting after meeting because of this new, weird friend of hers, Ashley Wyeth. Thank heavens, Claudia has gotten over all that and is a normal club member again. And Dawn is back to her alternate officer status.

There are also two associate members of the Baby-sitters Club — Logan Bruno (a boy!) and Shannon Kilbourne. But they don't come to our meetings. We just phone them for help when we get too busy.

I was the first club member to reach Claudia's

house that afternoon, which was fine with me because it would give the two of us a few more minutes to talk about what a jerk Howie Johnson is. I am so glad Claudia is my best friend. We've only known each other for a little over a year, because my parents and I lived in New York until then, but as soon as I moved to Connecticut we became friends. We are amazingly different, yet amazingly alike. For instance, Claudia is Japanese-American. Both of her parents were born in Japan. I'm just American. Well, technically I guess I'm Scottish-American and French-American, but you have to go back pretty far on either side of my family to find someone who actually lived in Scotland or France. Plus, Claudia is a terrible student but a great artist, and I'm a good student, but I don't know a thing about art.

On the other hand, Claudia and I are both sort of sophisticated. We've been interested in boys much longer than anyone else in the club, and we like to dress in wild, flashy clothes. Actually, Claudia may be a little wilder and flashier than I am, but our taste is about the same.

We were just deciding that Dorianne Wallingford is as big a jerk as Howie is when the doorbell rang and a few moments later, the rest of the club members came thundering upstairs. Kristy was first. She was wearing what I've come to think of as her Kristy uniform — jeans, sneakers, a turtleneck, and a sweater. That's the only kind of outfit she wears these days. She was followed by Mary Anne (who's Kristy's best friend), dressed slightly better in a jean skirt and an oversized sweat shirt. Kristy and Mary Anne remind me of a pair of magnets. They stick together even though they are as different as the opposite magnetic poles. Kristy is loud and outgoing and Mary Anne is quiet and shy. (She's sensitive, a good person to talk to if you have a problem.) They do have their similarities, though. They're both small for their age, and they're both a little less mature than Claudia and I. And Mary Anne is just beginning to be interested in clothes. (Kristy still couldn't care less.) Also, Mary Anne has a boyfriend — Logan Bruno, our associate club member. Kristy has never had a boyfriend, or even really liked a boy.

Last to run up the stairs was Dawn. She's our newest club member. Her mother moved her and her brother here from California after her parents got divorced. Dawn is an individual. She does things her way and doesn't care much about what other people think. She and Mary Anne are good friends, which is how

Dawn became a member of the club. Dawn has the longest, palest blonde hair I've ever seen in my life.

Since Kristy is a get-down-to-business sort of person, she immediately put on her visor, settled herself in Claudia's director's chair, and called our meeting to order. I announced how much money was in our treasury. Then, "Have you guys all been keeping up with the club notebook?" Kristy asked.

The club notebook is another of Kristy's big ideas. It's a good one, I guess, but it's kind of a pain, too. In the notebook, each of us is supposed to write up every single job we go on, and tell what happened and how the kids behaved and stuff. Then we're supposed to read the book at least once a week to find out what's happened on the jobs our friends have taken. This is helpful, but it sure uses up a lot of time.

We assured Kristy that we'd been reading the notebook. Then Claudia passed around some of the junk food she keeps hidden in her room, most of which I can't eat. I settled for some pretzels.

And then the phone began to ring — my favorite part of each meeting! People call us needing sitters, and we divide the jobs up according to who's free. It was a good day.

The phone rang six times, and we each got one job, except for Dawn, who wound up with two. My job was with Charlotte Johanssen.

Our meetings end at six o'clock, but that evening we all sat around a few minutes longer. Even Mary Anne did, and she usually rushes right home to start dinner for her and her father. At 6:05, the phone rang again.

"A late job call?" I wondered aloud. "It's a good thing we're still here." I picked up the phone since I was sitting closest to it. "Hello, Baby-sitters Club. . . . Oh, hi, Mom." (Why was my mother calling?)

"Honey," said Mom, "would you please come on home? You're late."

"It's only five after six," I pointed out. I usually haven't even reached my house by five after six.

"I'd like you to hurry home," she said firmly.

Something in her voice made my heart leap into my mouth, "Okay," I said, feeling scared. "I'll be right there. 'Bye." I hung up. "I have to go, you guys," I told my friends. "I don't know what it is, but something's wrong."

Before they did, something exciting occurred to me.

"Hey, Mom, are you pregnant? You *are,* aren't you?" I exclaimed. My parents always wanted to have another kid after they had me, but they hadn't been able to. Maybe I was finally going to be a big sister.

Dad smiled ruefully. "I wish that were the truth," he said, "but it isn't. I think I better tell you what's really going on before you imagine us colonizing Mars or something."

I giggled.

"All right," he went on. "This is the truth. Do you remember when my company opened the branch in Stamford?"

"Yes," I replied. "Right before we moved here."

Dad nodded. "Well, the new branch isn't doing well at all. The company has decided to get rid of it —"

"Oh, no! You lost your job!" I cried. Frantically, I began to calculate how much money I had saved from baby-sitting jobs, and how far it could be stretched.

"Not quite," said Dad. "They're combining the Stamford branch with the Boston branch. And I'm being transferred back to New York."

After I dropped my knife onto my plate, a silence fell over the room. The room, in fact, became so silent that I could hear the Marshalls' dog barking two houses away.

"Stacey?" said my mom gently. "We know this is a surprise, but think how much you've missed New York."

"I know, I know. I am thinking about that." I really *had* missed New York, even though my last few months there had been pretty unhappy, what with doctor visits, and friends who'd become *former* friends, and even a couple of stays in the hospital. On the other hand, I liked Stoneybrook a lot. I didn't have any former friends here, only true, good friends — except for Howie and Dori, the Jerk Twins. And I had the Baby-sitters Club and Charlotte Johanssen and a school I liked and a whole big house, instead of a not-so-big, tenth-floor apartment.

"Think of all the wonderful things we'll have when we move back to the city," said my father. "Lincoln Center and the Metropolitan Museum of Art."

"Central Park and the Donnell Library," added my mother.

"Bloomingdale's, Saks, Tiffany's, Benetton, Laura Ashley, Ann Taylor, Bonwit Teller, Bergdorf Goodman, and B. Altman's," I added, wondering if my parents would decide I was old enough to get some charge cards.

Mom and Dad laughed.

"That's the spirit," said my mother. "Eat your salad." (She watches me like a hawk, to make sure I stick *exactly* to my special diet.)

I ate a mouthful of salad, and, for good measure, one of chicken. "When are we moving? I hope it's at the end of the school year. I'm really looking forward to graduating with Claudia."

My parents glanced at each other.

"I'm afraid we can't possibly wait that long," my father told me. "The end of the school year isn't for months. We'll be back in New York four or five weeks from now."

"Four or five *weeks?!*" For the second time that night, I dropped my knife onto my plate.

"The company wants me back as soon as possible," said Dad, "and I plan to do what they ask. I feel lucky that we don't have to pick up and move to Boston."

"We put the house on the market today," Mom informed me, "and we've got real estate agents looking for an apartment in New York. We're going to try to move back to the neighborhood we were in before. That way you'll be near Laine again. Oh, and I talked to Miss Chardon at Parker Academy. You'll be able to rejoin your class there."

I couldn't believe it. My head was spinning.

Should I jump for joy and call Laine with the great news, or burst into tears and call Claudia with the rotten news?

Mom and Dad took my silence for shock and rushed ahead with more promises.

"We're going to try to find a bigger apartment," said my mother.

"We'll buy tickets to a show once a month," said my father.

"Claudia can visit you anytime."

"You can visit her anytime."

My excitement was growing. It was taking over any other feelings. I remember how I liked to walk down New York streets, and I could almost feel the city pulsing around me. It was noisy and busy and fast. There was something going on in New York at all hours of the day and night. In our old apartment, when I looked out of my bedroom window at night, I could see the city spread out before me, a maze of lighted windows. When I look out my window here at night, I see, well, darkness. Plus, there's not a thing to do in Stoneybrook after 10 p.m.

"Mom? Dad? This is great!" I cried. "Can I call Laine?"

My parents grinned.

"You can call her when you've finished your dinner," said Mom.

I never ate a meal so fast in my life. In a flash I was upstairs in my bedroom. I have a phone in my room, just like Claudia does, but I don't have a private number. I dialed Laine.

"Hi!" I said. "It's Stacey. You will never in a million years guess what I have to tell you."

"What?" screeched Laine.

I gave her the news.

She screeched some more. Then we began to talk and make plans about my return to New York. "I'll even be back in our class at Parker," I told her.

Laine paused. "You will?"

"Yeah. . . . Why?"

"Well, I don't know. I was just thinking about when you left. I mean, Allison Ritz and Val Schirmer and all those girls who, um —"

"Who hated me," I finished for her. I began to feel slightly numb. Who was I kidding? I'd been dying to get away from New York and all those former friends by the time we moved to Stoneybrook. How could I have forgotten about that? Here in Connecticut I had Claudia and Mary Anne and Dawn and Kristy, real friends who liked me and didn't care that I had diabetes.

"Laine," I said, "I better go. I'll call you again soon, okay? . . . Thanks. . . . 'Bye." I depressed the button on the phone and then dialed Claudia's number. "Hi, Claud," I said when she'd answered, and immediately I began to cry.

"What is it? What's wrong, Stace?" she kept asking.

When I finally managed to give her the news, Claudia began to cry, too.

"I have to see you," I told her. "I have to talk to you right now. Do you think I could come over even though it's a school night?"

"I'll check with my parents," Claudia said, "And you check with yours."

Ten minutes later, I was on my way back to the Kishis'.

CHAPTER 3

I was greeted at the door by the entire Kishi family, which was a little embarrassing since my eyes were red and puffy and my nose was all stuffed up.

I guess Claudia had told them my news right away. As soon as the door closed behind me, Mimi, Claudia's grandmother, gave me a gentle hug. "Such news!" she said with her soft accent. "Claudia will miss. We all will." (Mimi had a stroke last summer and it affected her speech. Although she's fairly well now, she still mixes up her words sometimes or leaves things out.)

"I can't believe you're going back to New York," said Janine, Claudia's older sister. "Well, of course, I can be*lieve* it, but the news was quite a shock." (Janine is really smart and speaks very precisely.)

Claudia's parents offered me a cup of tea, but I stared at Claudia, trying to send her a message with my eyes. It must have worked, because Claudia said, "Mom, Dad — Stacey and I want to go up to my room. We have a lot to talk about."

"All right," replied Mrs. Kishi. "We understand."

So Claudia and I closed ourselves into her bedroom. We sat side by side on her bed, with Lennie, her rag doll, between us. I held one of Lennie's yarn braids in my hands and began to unravel it.

"Um, Stace, this may sound silly, but I have to ask you this anyway," said Claudia. "Are you *really* moving back to New York? This isn't some big joke, is it?"

"Not unless Mom and Dad are pulling one over on me," I answered. "And that's not at all like them."

"You're moving in a *month?* I just can't . . . I don't know." Claudia's eyes filled with tears.

That was all it took to start *me* crying again. "I don't want to leave here," I wailed. "I *like* it here. I'm happy. There aren't any green lawns in New York. . . . *You* aren't in New York."

Claudia had bent over and was crying into her lap. She looked worse than I felt. "Hey, Claud," I said. "It's going to be okay. We can still visit each other."

20

"It's not the same. It isn't the same at all."

How come I was the one who was moving and Claudia was the one who looked hysterical? I reached over and touched her shoulder. "Calm down. Think about me. I'm the one who has to pack up her room, talk to her teachers . . . quit the Baby-sitters Club."

Claudia's sobbing grew louder.

"Shh," I said. "Your parents are going to think we're fighting or something. Claud, is anything *else* wrong? I mean, besides the fact that I'm moving?"

Claudia finally raised her head. She brushed her long hair out of her eyes, and I caught sight of her earrings, which were dangly little teddy bears. "Isn't that enough?" she replied. "Stace, I don't know if I ever told you this, but . . ." Her voice trailed away, and I could tell she was working up to some big confession, maybe still deciding if she really wanted to tell me whatever it was.

"Yes?" I prompted her. I'd stopped crying myself, because I was so wrapped up in Claudia. And I was really hoping she'd go ahead with what she had to say. If she stopped now, it would drive me crazy. It would be like when a little kid dances around, singing, "I know a secret!" and won't tell you what it is.

Claudia cleared her throat. "You," she told

me seriously, "are the only best friend I've ever had. What am I going to do without you?"

"*I've* been your *only* best friend? But you just met me a year ago."

Claudia nodded miserably.

I thought about things. Why hadn't I realized this? I should have. When the Baby-sitters Club first began, there were just four members — Claudia, Kristy, Mary Anne, and me. And I had known then that Kristy and Mary Anne were already best friends, and that even though they'd grown up right across the street from Claudia, neither of them was her best friend. But I became Claudia's best friend quickly. I guess I'd just assumed that over the years, Claudia had had some other best friends even though I didn't know anything about them. I mean, I'd had Laine, and in second grade there was Erin Tuki, and in kindergarten Missy Manheim, and in nursery school . . .

"How come you never had a best friend?" I asked Claudia.

She shrugged. "I always felt different from the other kids. Older, I guess. You know, it wasn't so long ago that Kristy and Mary Anne were still dressing up stuffed animals, but I gave that up in third grade. I was always taking art classes or trying out new things with my hair or experimenting with makeup. I just felt worlds apart from the other kids in my grade."

"And then I came along," I said.

"Right. And you were just like me. When I said something, you knew exactly what I meant. We liked the same movies, we had the same feelings about things. You know, sometimes I think I can read your mind."

"What am I thinking right now?" I asked.

Claudia frowned. "You're trying to think of some way to stay here in Stoneybrook," she said slowly.

"That's right!" I exclaimed.

"I knew it!" said Claudia. She actually smiled at me.

"Claud," I said suddenly. I put Lennie down and turned to face her, grabbing her hand. "Maybe I really could stay here."

Claudia brightened. "How?"

"Maybe Dad could look for a new job here or in Stamford. My parents are happy in Connecticut, too."

"Do you really think he'd do that?" asked Claudia excitedly.

"No."

"Oh. Maybe your dad could commute to New York, but your family could stay here."

"No. Too far."

"Oh."

"Hey!" I cried. "I asked my parents if we

could at least put the move off until eighth grade is over so I could graduate from Stoneybrook Middle School. And they said no, that was much too long to wait. But maybe . . ."

"WHAT?"

"Maybe Mom and Dad could move and I could stay here, at least until the school year's over. Or maybe even through the summer."

"Stay here?" I could see the gleam in Claudia's eyes. She knew what I meant. "Move in with us!" she exclaimed. "Oh, great! You could live in the guest bedroom. It would be super! We could do our homework together every night."

"I'd be right here for all the meetings of the Baby-sitters Club."

"We could try on makeup together."

"Go shopping together."

"We'd *never* get tired of each other."

"No, never!"

"Listen," said Claud. "Why don't I go downstairs and ask my parents and you stay here and call your parents? I bet it'll only take a few minutes to work things out. Later, everyone can get together to discuss the details."

"Okay!" I cried.

Claudia was right. It only took a few minutes — for all four of our parents to give us flat-out no's.

"What'd your parents say?" Claudia asked when she returned glumly to her room.

"They said they think you're wonderful but they need to be around to watch my diet and to take me to the doctor regularly, and that your parents have their hands full taking Mimi to physical therapy, and besides, Mom and Dad would miss me. What'd *your* parents say?"

"They said they think you're terrific but what about your diabetes, and they have their hands full with Mimi, and besides, wouldn't your parents miss you?"

I nodded. "It figures."

"Well, now what?" Claudia asked.

"I don't know."

We sat on her bed again.

"My parents are going to look for a bigger apartment. Maybe it will overlook Central Park," I said hopefully. "Anyway, there'll be plenty of room for you."

"Do you ever go to concerts in the park?" asked Claudia.

"Sure. Sometimes. And at Madison Square Garden."

"What's your favorite store in all of New York?"

"Oh, easy. Bloomingdale's. It's much better than the one in Stamford. We'll go there when you come visit."

"Can we go to a concert, too?"

"Sure."

"And to the Museum of Modern Art?"

"Anything."

"Maybe this won't be so bad after all," said Claudia.

"Maybe. . . . The only things I won't have are you and my friends."

"And green lawns."

"And peace and quiet."

"And Stoneybrook Middle School."

"And — the Baby-sitters Club."

Claudia and I looked at each other, and for a second I was sure we were both going to burst into tears again. "I'll have to tell Kristy and the others. I'll have to leave the club. You guys won't have a treasurer anymore."

"The club needs you," Claudia said softly. "Badly. We're too busy with five members. How will we get along with only four?"

"I better phone Kristy," I said. "We'll have to have an emergency club meeting as soon as possible. I guess tomorrow at lunchtime."

Claudia nodded. Then she picked up her phone and handed it to me.

I dialed it with shaking fingers. "Hello, Kristy?" I said. "It's Stacey. Emergency club meeting tomorrow in the cafeteria."

CHAPTER 4

I managed not to tell Kristy, Mary Anne, or Dawn the news about my move until we were actually sitting at our usual spot in the cafeteria with our food in front of us. That morning, Mom had taken pity on me and driven me to school (I usually walk with Claudia and Mary Anne), and then somehow I just hadn't seen any of my friends until lunch.

By the time fifth period rolled around, Kristy was so curious about the emergency meeting that she hustled everyone through the lunch lines and didn't even bother to make gross comments about the hot lunch, which she and Mary Anne always buy. Usually she sits at the table for a few minutes saying stuff like, "I've got it! Fungus — that's what this salad smells like!" or "Remember those gym socks I lost last week? I think they're right here in my succotash." She says these things to bug us,

27

but when she *didn't* say anything on the day of the emergency meeting, I suddenly realized that I would really miss Kristy and her comments after I left Stoneybrook.

"So," said Kristy briskly the second we were settled, "why did you call this meeting, Stacey?"

"Well, I called it because I have to tell you guys some very important news, and it's going to affect the club."

I looked around at the four faces that were watching me intently: Mary Anne's serious one, framed by her wavy, brown hair; Kristy, just as serious, chewing on the end of a pen; Dawn, her pale blue eyes wide with curiosity; and Claudia, exotic as ever, looking pained because she knew what was coming.

I cleared my throat. "I have to . . . You're not going to like this news."

"Are you sick?" asked Mary Anne suddenly. "Do you have to go into the hospital?"

"Oh, no," I replied hastily. "I —"

"Did something happen to one of your parents? Wait! No, don't tell me. They're getting divorced, right?" said Kristy, who knows much too much about such things. Like Dawn, Kristy's parents are divorced, only it wasn't a very nice divorce and Kristy never hears from her real father. But things are getting better for her. Last summer her mother remarried this rich guy, Watson Brewer. That's why Kristy doesn't live in our neighborhood anymore. She and her older brothers, Charlie and Sam, her little brother, David Michael, and her mom moved into Watson's mansion across town. Kristy is so lucky because in the process she acquired an adorable stepsister and stepbrother, Karen and Andrew, who live there part-time. (The rest of the time they live with their mother.)

"No, it's not a divorce," I told Kristy.

"Are you —" Dawn began.

But Claudia interrupted her. "Just let her talk, okay?" she said crossly.

"Okay, okay," said the others.

"We're moving," I said flatly. "Back to New York. In a month."

When Mom and Dad had told me the news, the kitchen had become silent. My friends' reaction was noisy.

"*Moving!*" exploded Kristy. "You can't move!"

"Why are you moving?" Dawn demanded to know.

"Aughh!" shrieked Mary Anne in a much louder voice than usual. "You're not! I don't believe it!"

"We are," I said, willing myself not to cry.

"Dad's company is transferring him. And it's definite. My parents like Connecticut, but they like New York, too. They've already put our house up for sale and they're looking for an apartment in the city. Everything's going to happen really fast."

If we hadn't been sitting smack in the center of the Stoneybrook Middle School cafeteria, I'm sure all five of us would have started wailing away. As it was, we were pretty close. Mary Anne (who cries easily) picked up her napkin and kept touching it to the corners of her eyes. Dawn put her fork down and began swallowing hard. Kristy (who rarely cries) bit her lip and stared out the window. I didn't do anything except *not* look at Claudia, but even so I knew she was not looking at me, too.

After a moment I said, "Your enthusiasm is underwhelming."

That brought a few smiles, at least.

Finally Kristy said, "I just can't believe it. You've only been here for . . ."

"A little over a year," I supplied.

Suddenly everyone had questions.

"Where will you go to school?" asked Dawn.

"Are you moving into your old apartment building?" asked Mary Anne.

"Will your parents let you come back here to visit?" asked Kristy.

I answered the questions, plus a few more. Claudia was nearly silent the whole time.

Then Kristy said, "Remember that night you baby-sat for Charlotte and there was a blackout?"

"Oh, yeah!" I replied, almost laughing. "And we heard noises in the basement, only they turned out to be Carrot." (Carrot is Charlotte's dog.)

"And remember when you took Kristy's cousins to the movies and they behaved like monsters?" said Dawn.

"I'll never forget it. What an afternoon."

"And when we were baby-sitting for all the Pike kids at the beach," added Mary Anne, "and we took them to play miniature golf?"

"That was the worst!" I cried. I glanced at Claudia.

"Remember when we met each other?" she managed to say.

"Of course. First day of school last year. I dropped my notebook and you stepped on it."

"By accident," she reminded me. "And then we looked at each other and we were both wearing off-the-shoulder sweat shirts and high-top sneakers."

"I couldn't decide whether to hate you or hope you'd become my best friend," I admitted.

"Same here," she said.

I looked at my watch. "Uh-oh! I have to go. I have to talk to Mr. Zizmore. He knows I'm moving, and he wants to go over some math with me. I might be able to skip into algebra back at my old school. Well, 'bye!" I jumped up. I just didn't want to face any more comments about leaving the Baby-sitters Club or about what good friends we'd all been. It would be too, too sad. And I couldn't talk to Mr. Zizmore if I was crying.

I didn't find this out until much later when Claudia told me (she tells me everything), but after I left the table, my friends continued to talk about me and the move.

"You know," said Claudia, "we really have to give Stacey a going-away party."

"A spectacular one," added Kristy. "Or at least a special one. Not just the five of us sitting around with soda and potato chips in club headquarters."

"What could we do that would be really special?" mused Mary Anne.

"A surprise party?" suggested Dawn.

"A big party with kids from school?" suggested Kristy, adding tentatively, "Boys . . . ?"

"Maybe," said Claudia, "but I'm not sure how special those ideas are."

"I know," agreed Kristy. "They're just regular old party ideas."

"We may have a little problem," Mary Anne spoke up.

"What?" asked Kristy.

"Well, I don't know about you guys, but I'm kind of low on money, and I don't think we should use treasury funds since Stacey contributes to the treasury, and it would be like she was paying for her own party. I've got about five dollars, myself."

"Oh," said Dawn. 'I've got five-fifty."

"I've got six," said Kristy. She looked at Claudia.

"Zero," replied Claud. "I just bought a new pair of sneakers."

"Sixteen-fifty won't go very far if we want to give Stacey a really special party," Dawn pointed out.

"That's not our only problem," said Kristy. "We're forgetting something. What on earth is the club going to do without Stacey? I know it's kind of mean to think about that right now, but it *is* a problem. A big one."

"Yeah," said Mary Anne slowly.

"I mean, we did all that advertising when school started," Kristy went on. "We got new customers — the Rodowskys, the Papadakises, the Delaneys, and everyone."

"And we depend on Logan and Shannon for help pretty often," added Dawn. "Hey, maybe one of them —"

"No, we've been through that already," Kristy interrupted. "They don't want to be regular members."

My friends grew silent, thinking.

"This is one big problem," said Kristy, heaving a sigh. "Being a member of the club takes up an awful lot of time."

"And we need someone just as responsible as Stacey," said Dawn.

"She is not going to be easy to replace," Kristy remarked. "Not at all. This may be the biggest problem our club has ever faced."

Meanwhile, I was upstairs with Mr. Zizmore. He was patiently explaining a problem to me, and I was patiently not listening. I was thinking of moving, of Claudia, of Laine, of the Jerk Twins, of awful Allison Ritz, of the Baby-sitters Club, of Charlotte Johanssen.

Charlotte. How could I tell her I was leaving? That her favorite person in the world was abandoning her? It wasn't my fault, but she wouldn't care whose fault it was. All she'd care was that I wouldn't be around anymore.

Of course, she had Carrot and all her best

friends, and she liked school. But I couldn't kid myself. She would really miss me. And I would miss her. And telling her I was leaving was going to be very, very hard.

Darn Dad and his stupid old company. They were making life miserable for a whole lot of people.

CHAPTER 5

Tonight I baby-sat for Jeff Schafer, and we had some discussion. Dawn, you'll especially be interested in it, but I hope it won't upset you when I talk to you about it tomorrow.

The evening got off to a bad start. As soon as you and your mom left, Jeff closed himself into his bedroom. (I guess that isn't so unusual these days.) Anyway, I didn't have much to do, so I sort of wandered around your house. I noticed the living room was a little messy (sorry, but it was), and I started picking things up and putting them away. Everything would have been okay if I hadn't decided to look at one of these pieces of crumpled-up notebook paper that was everywhere. But I did, and Jeff came downstairs just in time to see me. Boy, did he blow up!...

Mary Anne's job sitting for Jeff Schafer started out normally. Mary Anne was prepared for a fairly easy job since Jeff was the only kid to sit for, he's pretty old, and it was a school night, so she figured he'd have homework to keep him busy. She arrived at the Schafers' a little early. The reason Dawn wasn't taking care of her own brother was that she was going out with her mother. The public library was giving a program on old homes and "haunted" houses in Stoneybrook. This sort of thing is fascinating to Dawn. She loves to read ghost stories, and the Schafers' house is really old and even has a true secret passage in it. Of course, Mrs. Schafer and Dawn had asked Jeff to go to the lecture and slide show with them, but he'd refused. So Mary Anne was baby-sitting.

Ding-dong. Mary Anne could hear the Schafers' bell ringing in the house. It was followed by silence. At the Pikes' it's followed by the sound of a stampede as the eight kids run to the door. At the Perkins' it's followed by the frantic barking of Chewbacca, their dog. But at the Schafers' that night, Mary Anne didn't hear a thing. She was about to ring again when the door was flung open by Dawn.

"Sorry!" she apologized breathlessly. "You're

early! Mom and I were upstairs changing our clothes. Don't ask me why Jeff couldn't come to the door."

"Is he in one of his moods again?" Mary Anne asked warily.

Dawn nodded ruefully. "I guess so."

Mary Anne sighed. She knew that Jeff was having problems and had become sort of a handful since school began that fall. See, Dawn's parents got divorced almost a year ago, and Dawn and Jeff and their mom moved to Connecticut last January. (The reason they moved all the way to Stoneybrook from California is that Dawn's mother grew up here.) At first, things seemed to be going pretty smoothly. The Schafers got all the hard stuff out of the way. They found a house they liked, Dawn and Jeff started in their new schools, and finally Mrs. Schafer even got a job. Then, toward the end of the summer, Dawn and Jeff went to California to visit their father for the first time since they'd moved east. Dawn thought the trip went well, but maybe it went *too* well for Jeff. Not long after they returned to Stoneybrook, Jeff started acting cross and moody. In school he became a troublemaker. And lately he's been talking about moving back to his dad's, if that's possible. Dawn, of course, is praying it isn't. She doesn't want her family ripped in half.

Mary Anne stepped inside and Dawn closed the door behind her. Mary Anne really likes the Schafers' old house. The rooms are small and dark, the doorways are low, and the stairways are narrow. This may sound spooky and gloomy (and maybe it is), but Mary Anne loves the idea that the house is so old, and that all sorts of history has gone on while it was standing.

"I bet Jeff didn't want me to baby-sit, did he?" Mary Anne whispered to Dawn.

Dawn shook her head. (It's not that Jeff doesn't like Mary Anne. The problem is that he thinks he's old enough to be left alone. His mother agrees that he's old enough to be left alone during the day, but not at night.)

"Oh, well," said Mary Anne. "I'll live. Anyway, I came over early to see if you have any ideas about Stacey's party, or about getting money so we can give the party."

Dawn screwed up her face as she buttoned the last two buttons on her shirt and fastened an earring to one of her ears. "I really don't," she said at last. "How about you?"

"Not one single teeny idea," replied Mary Anne.

"Well, we'll just have to keep thinking," said Dawn philosophically.

"Dawn? Are you ready, honey?"

Mrs. Schafer called this out as she came thumping down the stairs, trying to put on her watch and straighten out her skirt at the same time. Mrs. Schafer is totally scatterbrained and disorganized, but she's really nice.

"I'm ready," Dawn replied.

"But you've only got one earring on," Mary Anne pointed out.

"Oh, I know." Dawn fingered the little pair of sunglasses that was hanging from her right ear. "This is the new style." Dawn is not quite as trendy as Claudia or me, but she's certainly more trendy than Kristy or Mary Anne, so if Dawn said one earring was in, Mary Anne believed her.

Mrs. Schafer and Dawn left for the library in a flurry of excitement. " 'Bye!" they called to Jeff as they dashed out to the car. They couldn't hear it, but Jeff's reply was the slamming of his bedroom door.

Mary Anne went upstairs and knocked on the door. "Jeff?" she called. "It's me, Mary Anne. I'll be here until your mom and Dawn come back."

No answer.

"Let me know if you need help with your homework or anything."

No answer.

"Come down later and I'll fix you a snack."

No answer.

Mary Anne went back down the stairs. She'd finished her homework that afternoon, so there wasn't much for her to do except watch TV. She wandered into the kitchen and looked at the big brick fireplace that had been built in colonial days. She wandered into the dining room and glanced outside through the wobbly panes of glass in the window. Then she wandered into the living room and discovered the mess that she'd written about in the club notebook. A can of creamed spinach was sitting on the couch, and a screwdriver and a doormat had been tossed into a corner. (I told you Mrs. Schafer is scatterbrained.) Plus, the floor was littered with crumpled-up papers.

Mary Anne put the doormat and screwdriver in the garage, and the spinach in the kitchen, and returned to the living room with a plastic garbage bag. She began tossing the papers in the bag. About halfway through the job, she glanced idly at one piece of paper that was hardly scrunched up at all. This is what she saw:

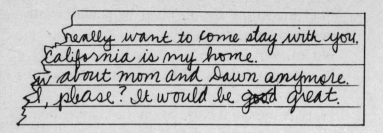

really want to come stay with you.
California is my home.
about mom and Dawn anymore.
, please? It would be ~~good~~ great.

"What do you think you're doing?"

Mary Anne jumped and turned around. She found Jeff standing behind her, his face red with anger.

"I was just — just cleaning up," Mary Anne replied guiltily, but she knew it didn't look that way to Jeff.

"You were not just cleaning up. You were reading my stuff. I was trying to write a letter. Mail is private, you know. It's a federal offense to read someone else's mail."

Jeff's mouth twitched and Mary Anne thought he might cry. Between that and his blond hair hanging in his eyes, he suddenly looked like a very little boy.

"I'm sorry if I upset you," Mary Anne said. "I guess I *was* reading your letter, but I didn't mean to snoop. These papers were just lying here on the floor."

Jeff reached over and snatched the letter out

of Mary Anne's hand. He started to stomp back up to his room.

"You know," said Mary Anne, thinking fast, "Stacey McGill is moving back to New York City. That's where she used to live before she moved to Stoneybrook."

Jeff stopped in the middle of a stomp. He turned around and ran back down the stairs. "Really?" he said. "How come? Her parents aren't divorced, are they?"

Mary Anne shook her head. "Nope. Her father's company is transferring him. He has to move because of his job."

"Oh." Jeff dropped onto the couch, the picture of disappointment.

"Stacey really likes New York," Mary Anne went on. "She'll miss her friends here, but, well, I think deep down she's glad she's going back."

"I don't blame her," said Jeff miserably.

"You'd like to go back to California, wouldn't you?" Mary Anne asked him.

Jeff nodded.

"Do you really hate it here?"

Jeff was quiet for a long time. At last he said, "My dad needs me and I need him."

"Your mom and Dawn need you, too. And you need them."

"That's different. We left Dad all alone out in California. Besides, Mom and Dawn are girls. Dad and I are boys. . . . I hate girls! They treat me like a baby. Dad doesn't do that. And if I lived with Dad, Mom and Dawn would still have each other." Jeff looked at Mary Anne and then looked away quickly.

"My dad used to treat me like a *huge* baby," Mary Anne confided, "but I think he just did that because he loves me."

"Maybe," said Jeff slowly.

"Families belong together," said Mary Anne.

"Well, we're not together now. Dad's not with us."

"That's what happens when parents get divorced. But your family is more together now than it would be if you went back to California."

"I don't see how," said Jeff. "Apart is apart. Dad needs me. Mom has Dawn. She doesn't need both of us."

Mary Anne wasn't sure what to think. She could see Jeff's side of the problem, and Dawn's, too. She and Jeff talked for a long time that night.

The next day, Mary Anne and Dawn discussed everything in a whispered conversation during study hall. When the bell rang at the end of the period, Dawn looked at Mary Anne and shrugged. "I really don't know what's going to happen," she said, "but whether Jeff goes or stays, it's not going to be good. Somebody is going to get hurt."

CHAPTER 6

"I can't — oof — jam these in . . . any . . . *further!*"

"Here, let me help you." I ran into the den, where my mother was trying to close up a carton of books she'd just packed, and flung myself on the box.

"Stacey, that works with suitcases full of clothes, but not cartons full of books," my mother said. "I'll just have to take some of these out and start a new carton. Honestly, I thought twenty boxes would be more than enough to pack up the stuff in here. But I underestimated. I bet I've underestimated for every room in the house. How did we acquire so much stuff?"

I frowned, looking around the half-empty den. "When we moved here," I reminded Mom, "we thought the house looked empty, so we bought some things to fill it up. I guess we did a pretty good job."

"Far too good," Mom replied. "There is no way we're going to be able to fit everything we own into our new apartment."

"I thought the new apartment was bigger than the old one," I said.

"It is. But not big enough to hold a whole houseful of furniture and books and . . . and junk."

My mom was going a little crazy with the packing. She and Dad had found a nice, big apartment in New York, and we could move into it whenever we were ready, but we had run into a slight problem — how to cram a house into an apartment. Mom was right. There was no way.

"You know," I said, "there's probably a lot of stuff we don't really need. There's that old ironing board that doesn't work —"

"I don't know why I kept it after we got the new one."

"— and the crutches from the time Dad broke his foot —"

"I hope we'll never need those again."

"— and all the clothes I outgrew this year —"

"Somebody could use them. You grew so fast you barely wore them."

"— and all the stuff in the attic."

"Junk. Pure junk."

"Why don't we have a yard sale?" I suggested.

"I don't think so, honey."

"But everyone in Connecticut has yard sales. You see the signs all over the place."

"Oh, I know. But how can I possibly arrange for a yard sale when I have to pack and send out change-of-address cards and call the real estate people, the phone company, the electric company, the —"

"What if I ran the sale?" I interrupted. "I bet my friends would help me. It would be fun."

"We-ell," said Mom slowly. "It's a big job, you know. You have to price everything and tag all the items and organize them and set them up in the yard. And advertise."

"Mom, Mom, relax. You're giving me a headache. My friends and I could do it. I know we could."

My mother, who had been crouching on the floor, rocked back on her heels. She blew a strand of hair out of her face, then glanced around the room at the overflowing cartons and the cupboards full of stuff we hadn't even looked at yet. "Stacey," she said at last, "I would love to weed out the things we don't need anymore. If you and your friends will organize and run the entire sale, you can keep whatever money you make."

"Are you kidding?!" I cried. "Oh, thanks! It might be a lot of money, though, Mom. All those little things add up."

"It's yours. It'll be worth it to your father and me. If we don't get rid of this stuff now, we'll just have to do it after we get to New York and find that there's no room for it. And we won't be able to hold a yard sale in the middle of the city."

"Oh, wow! Thanks! Great! Fantastic! Can I call the club members and tell them?"

Mom grinned. "Go ahead."

I dashed out of the den and up to my bedroom, where I grabbed the telephone. Who should I call first? It was a Saturday. My friends might be home, they might not.

I dialed Claudia.

"Guess what! Guess what!" I shrieked into the phone. "Oh. . . . Mimi? Sorry. It's Stacey. Didn't I dial Claudia's number? . . . Oh, okay. . . . Over at Mary Anne's? All right. I'll call her there. Thanks. 'Bye."

I called Mary Anne's house.

"Mary Anne! Mary Anne! Guess what. I've got amazing news!"

"You're not moving after all!" she cried.

In the background I could hear excited shrieks. "She's not moving? She's staying here?"

"Who's over there?" I asked. "I mean, besides Claudia?"

"Kristy," Mary Anne replied. "So how come you're not moving after all?"

"Oh, we're moving," I told her. "That's not the news."

"She's still moving," Mary Anne said to the others.

The shrieking stopped.

I told Mary Anne about the yard sale. "So even if we earn a whole lot of money, we get to keep it and divide it up five ways." I finished up.

"Wow, that's terrific," said Mary Anne.

"Tell the others," I instructed her. "I'll call Dawn."

"Oh, you don't have to do that. She's on her way over. Why don't you come over, too?"

"Okay!" At the time, I was so excited about the sale that I didn't even bother to wonder why the members of the club were getting together without having invited me to join them. I just hopped on my bike and rode over to the Spiers' house.

Mary Anne let me in and we ran up to her room. I was greeted by the sight of Kristy and

Claudia, both wearing visors and blowing pink bubbles, and Dawn over in a corner, standing on her head. Her hair had fallen in a blonde pool around her head, and her face was turning red. At the sight of me, Kristy and Claudia popped their bubbles and Dawn dropped to the floor.

"Your mom really said we could give a yard sale?" she cried.

"Yup," I replied, as Mary Anne and I sat on her bed.

"And keep the money?" Kristy asked.

(I saw Claudia elbow Kristy in the ribs.)

"Yup," I said again. "All of it. We'll split it five ways."

"I feel kind of funny taking money for selling *your* things," Mary Anne admitted. "Not that I couldn't use the money, but, I don't know. . . ."

"Listen, it's a favor to my parents," I insisted. I told them about the conversation I'd had with Mom.

"It *would* be fun," said Claudia. "I love yard sales. We can make posters to put up in the neighborhood. Everyone will come over."

"Yeah, I just love selling stuff," added Kristy.

"Oh, this is terrific!" I squealed. "I better go home. The only thing I'll need Mom's help with is weeding out the items for us to sell. Maybe she'll want to start right now. I'll see you guys later!"

I left Mary Anne's house, but the others stayed. Claudia told me later (after I'd moved, during one of our many marathon phone conversations) that the others had gathered at Mary Anne's to talk about the party (what else?), and where they were going to get enough money to give a good one.

"Well, I've been thinking and thinking," Claudia said, gazing out the window and watching me cross the Spiers' front yard, "and I just can't come up with an idea that's really special. You know, for a party that Stacey will never forget, and that will really *mean* something."

"Me, neither," said Kristy, Mary Anne, and Dawn.

"And now we've got another problem," said Mary Anne.

"What?" asked the rest of the club members.

"Well, don't you guys feel funny about taking money for selling the McGills' things? I do."

"I know what you mean," agreed Dawn, "unless . . . oh, we are so stupid! This solves two problems!"

"Unless what?" asked Kristy excitedly. "What solves which problems?"

"Unless we take the money we earn from the yard sale and use it to give Stacey her party! That solves the problem of getting enough money to give a good party *and* the problem of feeling like we're taking the McGills' money. I mean, because in a way we'll be giving it back to Stacey."

Kristy clapped her hand to her forehead. "You're right! We really *are* stupid! The answer to our money problems was practically staring us in the face!"

"Now," said Claudia, "the only problem left is — what kind of party should we give?"

"Yeah . . ." said Mary Anne.

And the four of them fell silent, thinking.

While they thought, I returned home and talked to my mother about the yard sale. She promised to help me sort through closets, the attic, and the basement the next day. Since I didn't have anything else except homework to do then, I got on the phone with Laine.

"Hi!" she cried. "Guess what! As a welcome-back present, my dad got tickets for you and me to go see *Mad About Millie*!"

"No!" I shrieked. "Really? Oh, that is fantastic!" *Mad About Millie* is this Broadway musical we've been dying to see. "What's going on in school?" I asked. "I'll be there with you in just a few weeks. Oh, and my math teacher is getting me ready to take algebra."

"Super. We'll be in the same class then. There's only one eighth-grade algebra class. . . . Allison Ritz is in it, too."

"She is? Has, um, she said anything about my coming back?"

"Well . . ." Laine cleared her throat. A long pause followed. "She sort of said, 'Oh, great, Barf-mouth is returning.' "

"Barf-mouth?"

"Yeah. From that time you got sick in the cafeteria. You know, when you were having those spells? Before you were on the insulin? You kind of threw up a little."

I groaned. I must have been really out of it when that happened. I didn't even remember it. But Allison sure did. Val Schirmer probably did, too. And all the rest of the kids I used to go to school with. "Maybe I should play dumb," I said, "so Mr. Zizmore will keep me out of algebra. Better yet, maybe I should ask Mom and Dad to put me in a different school."

"Stace, *no. I* want you in Parker Academy. And algebra."

"Oh, Laine." Just a minute ago, I'd felt happy and excited. Now I was sad and worried. Did I or didn't I want to leave Stoneybrook? Did I or didn't I want to go back to New York? I couldn't tell. It was all part of moving. Some good feelings, some bad ones, some happy, some sad.

I wished I could divide myself and live half in Stoneybrook, half in New York City.

CHAPTER 7

The Pike kids have a new game.
Its called SAs. (I think) SAs meant
secret Agents. You know, like spys.
Jordin is the head spy. Adam and
Byran are his top agents. The rest
of the Pikes are just reglar agents.
(Malary isnt a agent becuase she's
to old.) What the SAs do is spy on
there new nieghbers in the house
behind them. These paeple just
moved in and I guess they're a
little strang, but I'm sure there
not spys. Try telling that to the
Pikes though.

All us club members love to sit for the Pikes, even though there are eight of them and sometimes they get out of hand. In case you've forgotten about them, let me give you a rundown on the Pikes. The youngest is Claire. She's five. Then there's seven-year-old Margo, eight-year-old Nicky, nine-year-old Vanessa, the ten-year-old triplets (Byron, Jordan, and Adam), and last of all, Mallory, who's eleven.

Mallory has been a sort of junior baby-sitter for a while now. When us club members held a play group last summer, Mallory gave us a hand. And lately she's been the "second" sitter almost every time there's a job at the Pikes'. (Since there are eight children, Mrs. Pike usually likes to have two sitters in charge.)

Anyway, when Claudia went to sit at the Pikes' that afternoon, she had no idea what she was getting into. She thought she and Mallory would have just the usual Pike bedlam to put up with. But, no, Jordan had invented SA's.

"Where is everybody?" Claudia asked, as Mallory let her in the front door. She was used to being met by a herd of children.

"Out back," Mallory replied, rolling her eyes. "I'll explain as soon as Mom leaves."

Mrs. Pike bustled downstairs, giving last-minute instructions and phone numbers to Claudia and Mallory. Then she inched her station wagon down the driveway and was gone.

"Okay," said Mallory. "Come here." She led Claudia to the Pikes' back door. "Look in the yard. What do you see?"

"Nothing," Claudia replied.

"Look harder. Look in the elm tree, for instance."

Claudia squinted her eyes. She saw a pair of blue jeans and some curly hair. "Jordan?" she guessed.

"Right."

"What's he doing up there?"

"I'll tell you in a minute. See if you can find everyone else."

It took a while, but Claudia finally spotted Claire and Margo crouched behind a yew bush, Nicky lying flat on his stomach in some tall grass, Vanessa peeking around a corner of the toolshed, and Adam and Byron up an ash tree. There was not a sound in the Pikes' backyard.

"What are they doing?" Claudia whispered.

"Spying," Mallory replied. "And we don't have to whisper. They're playing a game called SA's. That stands for Secret Agents. Some people finally moved into the Congdons' house, and those goons — " (Mallory waved her hand, indicating her brothers and sisters) "— think the new people are foreign spies."

The Congdons' house sat just beyond the back edge of the Pikes' property. Adam and Byron in the ash tree were practically looking in the bedroom windows, that's how close they were to the house.

"Why do they think the new people are spies?" Claudia wanted to know.

"Oh, they have a long, funny last name, and they speak with accents. They sound like this: 'ow nize do meed you. Thank you zo moch for your 'ozpeetaleetee."

Claudia giggled. "Do they really sound like that?" she asked.

"They really do," Mallory replied. "But that doesn't mean they're spies."

This is what us sitters like about Mallory. She is totally levelheaded. And practical. And usually willing to give people the benefit of the doubt. Not that she doesn't have an imagination. She does. She loves to read and is usually in the middle of at least four books. She likes to write, too. And when she's alone, she daydreams. But when she's helping us baby-sit, she's always on top of things.

"We better go out there and see what they're up to," Claudia said, opening the door.

Mallory and Claudia strode through the

backyard. They were intending to keep an eye on the kids. Instead, they wound up helping with spy missions that afternoon.

"Psst! PSSST!" hissed a frantic voice.

The girls looked around. They found Jordan signaling to them from his tree. He was waving a little spiral notebook around.

"What?" asked Claudia and Mallory at the same time.

"Come here. And *keep quiet!*"

The girls tiptoed to the base of the elm tree. "What is it?" asked Claudia. "By the way, your mother left. She'll be back around five-thirty."

"Okay," said Jordan quickly. Apparently, Mrs. Pike was the furthest thing from his mind. "Listen, you gotta keep quiet. We don't want the spies to know *we're* spying on *them.*"

"Jordan, they are not spies," Mallory whispered.

"They might be. That's what we have to find out. You should see all the stuff that's in their den. There's a Xerox machine, a Telex machine, two computers, a printer —"

"How do you know?" Claudia asked.

"Vanessa looked in the window. She earned her yellow badge for that."

"Huh?"

"You have to complete certain missions,"

Mallory explained to Claudia. "Every time you do, you get a badge. Getting the pink badge is easiest. Black is hardest. And there are eight other badges in between. If you earn all ten, you're named a top agent, like Byron and Adam. They've been going on missions more often than anyone else."

"Would you guys be quiet?" asked Jordan. "Nicky's setting up the tape recorder. I don't want it to pick up your voices."

Claudia nearly fell over. "Tape recorder? What tape recorder?"

Jordan jumped out of the tree and led Claudia and Mallory toward the house. "We have to find out what they're talking about," he said.

"I think that's invasion of privacy," Claudia told him. "Isn't it?" She turned to Mallory.

"I don't know," Mallory replied, "but you guys are trespassing."

"We are not," said Jordan huffily. "We're not setting a toe on their property. At least not for this. Nicky's going to tape from up in a tree. And the tree's in our yard."

"Well, I hope he's careful," said Mallory. "The only one of us kids who's ever broken a bone is Nicky, and that was when he fell out of a tree."

Jordan looked slightly worried, but he held his ground. "He has to start climbing again

61

sometime. Besides, he's going to earn a green badge if he does a good job. Anyway, can you two give me a hand? I can't assign missions and help my agents *and* keep track of who's earned which badges. Here." Jordan thrust his notebook at Mallory. "Just make a note any time an agent gets a badge." Then he ran back to the elm tree.

Mallory opened the little notebook and Claudia peered inside. At the top of each page was the name of one of Jordan's "agents." Running down the side were the words *Pink, White, Yellow, Orange, Red, Purple, Green, Blue, Brown,* and *Black.* At least one color was checked off on each page. All the colors on Adam's and Byron's pages were checked off.

"Hey," said Mallory, grinning. "Jordan didn't bother to give himself a page, since he's head spy. He is so stuck-up. He invented the game, so he doesn't even have to go on any missions. He just sits in that tree and gives out orders."

Claudia smiled, too. Then she said, "Come on. I have a feeling we should check on Nicky. I don't want any broken bones."

"Or any inversion of privacy," added Mallory.

"Whatever." Claudia smiled. Mallory might be practical and levelheaded, but she *is* two years younger than Claudia and the rest of the club members.

The girls hunted Nicky down. Just as Jordan had said, he was perched in a tree a few yards from one of the bedroom windows of the new neighbors. He looked safe enough, though.

"Let's see what the others are up to," Claudia said, but before they'd gone very far, Claire came running over to them.

"Give me my white badge! Give me my white badge!" she cried.

From somewhere nearby, Jordan shushed her.

Claire lowered her voice to a whisper. "I sneaked all the way around to their front door. Then I rang the bell and hid. Jordan says I get my white badge for that."

"Okay," said Claudia.

Mallory put a check next to the word *White* on Claire's page. "What happened when the people answered their bell?" she asked.

"Only the lady came to the door," Claire told her. "She has long, long dark hair. It's even longer than Dawn Schafer's. And she looked around and around and said, " 'elloo? 'elloo? 'oo eez 'ere?' Then she went back inside."

Claudia and Mallory glanced at each other and shrugged.

The spying continued all afternoon. Margo rang the bell and hid, too, but Claudia had to tell the SA's to quit doing that. Vanessa spotted an open basement window and lay on the ground at the edge of the Pikes' yard looking in with a pair of binoculars. She didn't see anything but darkness, but she earned an orange badge for her quick thinking. At long last, Nicky climbed out of the tree with the tape recorder.

"Let's go inside and find out what they said," he suggested.

"Don't you know?" asked Mallory.

"Nope. I fell asleep."

The Pikes were tired of spying so they followed Nicky into the house. The first part of the tape was nothing but birds chirping and leaves rustling. Once, Nicky yawned. At long last, though, a voice was heard. Only one sentence was spoken and then a door slammed.

The voice said, "Ve vill have courgettes for deener." Then, *slam!*

"That just sounds like a regular old French accent," Claudia said, but nobody heard her. The kids were in a panic.

"Courgettes? What are courgettes?" shrieked the Pikes.

"Children?" suggested Nicky, with terror in his eyes.

There was confusion until Mallory thought to look up the word in a cookbook. "Courgettes," she informed everyone, "is the French word for zucchini. You know, squash?"

Claudia grinned. Mallory had saved the day. She had prevented hysteria. Thank goodness she was so practical.

Claudia told me later that as she walked home that evening, she thought about my moving. She thought about the hole I'd leave in the club. Could Mallory fill the hole? she wondered. No, she decided immediately. Mallory was good with kids, but she was two years younger than the rest of us sitters. How would she fit into the club? And she didn't have nearly as much experience as I did.

As Kristy had said, I was going to be hard to replace.

CHAPTER 8

need a toaster?
need a coaster?
never fuss --
come see us!

need a pail?
need a snail?
then be hasty --
Come see Stacey!

"What do you think?" asked Claudia, holding up some sample ads for our yard sale.

"Well," I said, trying to be tactful, "the art is wonderful, Claud. I love your snail with his antennae, and the house on his back instead of a shell. . . ."

"But?" Claudia prompted me.

I glanced at our other friends.

"But the poetry stinks," spoke up Kristy. "*Hasty* and *Stacey* don't rhyme, and we don't have any snails for sale."

"Well, thanks a lot," said Claudia huffily.

The members of the Baby-sitters Club were gathered, for the third afternoon in a row, at my house to get ready for the yard sale. Mom was right. A sale was a lot of work, but we'd been having fun. At least, we had been up until now.

"Hey, everybody," I said, "I don't want to be a slave driver or anything, but we don't really have time for arguments."

"But, Stacey, Kristy is so rude," Claudia complained, looking wounded.

"I'm sorry," Kristy said contritely. "Really I am. Look, why don't we divide up the work on the ads and each do what we're best at? Dawn and I will write the poems, Mary Anne and Stacey, you do the lettering, and Claudia, you illustrate the ads. . . . Nobody can draw as well as you," she added.

Claudia looked mollified. "All right," she agreed.

"And after we've made a few more good ads to put up," I said, "we better start tagging all that junk in the basement."

We bent over our papers and worked busily.

"Now *this* is an advertisement," Kristy announced a few minutes later. "Listen."

Here's what she read:

" 'We're moving back to New York City,
We know it's going to be hard.
But things will be just a little bit better,
If you'll come to the sale in our yard.' "

"Not bad," I agreed. "I like that. Mary Anne, let's each letter one of those poems."

"Okay," she said and set to work on a piece of bright yellow construction paper.

"All right, how's this?" said Dawn after a few more minutes. She brushed a strand of hair out of her eyes. Then, as if she were about to recite a composition in English class, she stood up, put her hands behind her back and said gravely, "Red are the roses, blue are the seas. . . . Come buy our junk. Please, please, please, please!"

For a moment, no one could tell whether

Dawn was joking or serious, but when we realized she was practically turning blue from trying not to laugh, we all began snickering and giggling. Dawn laughed the hardest of all.

"Very funny," I said, when we'd recovered. "Does anyone want something to drink?"

"Only if you've got some soda that's just brimming with sugar, caffeine, and sodium," replied Kristy. "And maybe some artificial coloring, and, oh, some bigludium exforbinate."

I laughed. "We've probably got something like that. I'm going to have iced tea, though."

"I'll have iced tea, too," said Dawn, who had turned green at the very thought of artificial coloring.

"I'll go for the glutious exorbitants," said Claudia.

"Me, too," said Mary Anne.

Claudia followed me to the kitchen and helped me fill five glasses. I'd noticed lately that when she and I were with the rest of the club, we acted happy or silly, and kidded around. But when we were alone we fell into a sad kind of silence. We weren't angry; we just had all these "last things" to say to each other but didn't know how to say them, which was maybe the saddest thing of all about my moving.

"You know," I said, dancing around the edge of the awful subject, "I haven't told Charlotte that I'm moving."

Claudia, who was standing by the ice-maker in the freezer, glanced over her shoulder at me. "You haven't?" she said in surprise.

I shook my head. "I guess I've been putting it off."

"You better tell her soon," said Claud. "I mean, the ads for the yard sale will be a major clue. Don't you think she should find out from you and not from some poem that begins 'Red are the roses, blue are the seas'?"

I smiled. "I guess so. It's not going to be easy, though."

"No, I suppose it isn't. If she feels anything like me . . ."

I waited for Claudia to finish her sentence, but she let it hang there.

"Well," I said, "we better go back upstairs. Kristy's waiting to be bigludium exforbinated."

Claudia just nodded. I thought she looked a little teary, but by the time we had joined the others, she seemed fine.

We worked on the ads until we had finished our soda and iced tea. We'd made quite a stack and were pretty proud of them.

"All right," I said. "Down to the basement.

Wait'll you guys see what Mom bought for us this morning."

"What? What?" cried my friends.

"You'll see," was all I'd tell them.

We reached the top of the steps to the basement and I flicked on the light. The sale items were downstairs in a big jumble on, under, and around the Ping-Pong table we'd bought the winter before and now had to sell.

"These," I said when the five of us were standing by the sale items, "are what my mom bought us." I held up two small packages from the dime store.

"What are they?" asked Mary Anne.

"Price tags. Blank ones." I replied. "Some that we can stick on, and some that we can tie on things we don't want to gum up, like stuffed animals or clothes."

"Oh, great!" exclaimed Kristy. "This sale is going to look so professional! Let's start the tagging right now."

"Okay." I took a sweater from off the pile of clothes I'd outgrown. "What do you guys think? Forty dollars?"

"*Forty!*" screeched Claudia. "Are you kidding?"

"Well, Mom must have paid a lot for it, and it's only a *year* old. Forty dollars is a steal."

"Not at a yard sale it isn't," said Mary Anne.

"Are you sure?" asked Dawn.

"Dawn, have you ever been to a yard sale?" asked Kristy.

"No. People in California don't have yard sales."

"Well, trust me; you put a forty-dollar tag on that sweater, and our customers will laugh us right out of the yard."

After a whole lot of haggling, my friends talked me down to $3.50. I was stunned. "How are we going to earn any money?" I asked.

"We will," Kristy insisted. "You'll see."

Finally, we got the hang of how much we could charge for things, so we divided up the items and set to work separately. The pricing went quickly that way. We'd gone through maybe a third of the stuff when, very slowly, Kristy raised her head and looked around at the rest of us. "Heyyy," she said softly in a way I knew meant she'd just had another one of her brilliant business ideas.

"What?" we asked.

"I have an idea."

(I knew it!)

"Let's make this sale more than just a regular yard sale. Let's sell lemonade, too."

"And how about those great brownies I can bake?" suggested Claudia.

"And — and handmade stuff," I suggested.

"Like potholders and scarves," said Mary Anne.

"What about babies from my spider plants?" said Dawn.

"Yeah!" cried the others.

"Oh, boy!" I exclaimed. "This yard sale is going to go down in yard-sale history as the best ever!"

"Stellar," agreed Kristy.

CHAPTER 9

You guys, I promise this notebook entry isn't a joke. If you don't believe what happened, you can ask Karen or Andrew about it. Or you can ask Morbidda Destiny herself. (But I know you never will!)

Anyway, I baby-sat for Karen and Andrew this afternoon. It was kind of an emergency. Watson's ex-wife got in a jam and needed a sitter for Karen and Andrew, so Watson asked if I'd mind taking care of them after school. Of course I didn't mind! They're almost like my real brother and sister, instead of my stepbrother and stepsister.

I wasn't silly enough to think that the job would be easy, though. And I was right. But it was so interesting that I didn't even mind that it was scary, too...

74

Interesting? Was Kristy kidding? Her baby-sitting job was so scary and weird that I get goosebumps all over whenever I think about it. The afternoon started off with about as much pandemonium as we usually find at the Pikes' house. After all, there were Kristy, Andrew, Karen, David Michael (Kristy's youngest brother, whom she was also supposed to be watching), Boo-Boo (Watson's cat), and Shannon (David Michael's puppy). Then Amanda and Max Delaney and Hannie and Linny Papadakis dropped by to play.

Let me just remind you about all those kids. Karen and Andrew are six and four, and David Michael is seven. Amanda and Max are eight and six. They're really Karen's friends, and don't always get along too well with David Michael. Linny and Hannie are also eight and six. Linny is David Michael's good friend, and Hannie is Karen's good friend. The Papadakis kids are friendly and easygoing and get along with anybody — except Amanda and Max. And Amanda and Max don't like Hannie and Linnie much, either. So there were a lot of "enemies" in this little crowd of kids.

But Kristy was dealing with the seven of them fairly well. For one thing, she insisted that they play outside in the backyard. Nobody minded. Shannon the puppy was more fun outside than inside. She would frisk after bugs and chase falling leaves and tumble around in the grass. Things were going so well that Kristy sat down in a lawn chair and simply watched the scene before her.

David Michael, Linny, and Andrew were trying to set up an obstacle course for Shannon — arranging stones and chairs for her to jump over, crawl through, and dive under. Kristy knew it would never work — and that the boys wouldn't really care.

The girls and Max were chasing poor Boo-Boo through the yard. What you need to remember about Boo-Boo is that he's fat and old. And pretty bad-tempered. Kristy and her family had been living in Watson's house for several whole months, and Kristy was not sure she'd ever even patted Boo-Boo. He was good for chasing, though. Kristy hoped the kids would tire Boo-Boo out and that he would go indoors and fall asleep. (Kristy liked Boo-Boo much better asleep than awake.)

"Boo-Boo! Boo-Boo!" Amanda called.

Boo-Boo had paused by a rosebush. Amanda made a move as if she were going to come after him again. It was a fake, though (just like in football), but Boo-Boo fell for it and ran up a tree, claws clinging wildly.

"I think Boo-Boo might be under another spell, you guys," Karen informed the others, and Kristy shook her head. Karen wasn't going to start that Morbidda Destiny stuff again — was she?

Yes, she was.

"A spell?" Hannie repeated, her eyes widening. "You mean — a witch's spell?" Hannie's gaze traveled across the yard to Mrs. Porter's house next door. The house was old, Victorian, with gables and turrets and towers. And it was run-down. It was a Halloween house.

"Yes," replied Karen. "I saw Morbidda Destiny with bottles and jars last weekend. I think she was working up some new potions."

Kristy wondered whether she should put a stop to Karen's stories. Often, she did. They sometimes got out of hand. However, David Michael, Linny, and Andrew were now listening, too, and everyone seemed just plain fascinated. Besides, if the stories kept the Papadakises from arguing with the Delaneys, and the Delaneys from being mean to David Michael, well . . .

Kristy let Karen go on. See, Karen thinks

that old Mrs. Porter, who lives alone in the Halloween house, is actually a witch named Morbidda Destiny, and that she mixes potions and brews, casts spells, rides a broomstick, and goes to witches' meetings. Mrs. Porter *is* a little strange, and she *does* dress in funny, long, black robes, but Kristy is fairly certain she isn't a witch. (She's never been able to convince Karen of that, though.)

"What kind of potions is she working up?" Max asked Karen.

"Witch potions."

"You mean . . . ?" Hannie began.

Karen nodded her head. "Yes. To turn people and animals into witches. To turn *us* into witches."

"Us?" shrieked Amanda. "Well, how could she ever get us to take the potions? We'd have to drink them, wouldn't we?"

"Yes," replied Karen."

"And we wouldn't be stupid enough to drink something Morbidda Destiny gave us, would we?"

Karen remained undaunted. "Witches have their ways," she said mysteriously.

All seven children turned wary eyes to Mrs. Porter's house, as if expecting to see a bat fly out a window or something. Of course, nothing happened.

Finally, David Michael said, "Well, now I'm thirsty. Kristy, can we make some lemonade?"

"I don't think we have any mix," she told her brother.

"Hey, could we make *real* lemonade?" asked Hannie, inspired. "It would be fun! All you need is lemons and water and sugar. And ice."

"It *would* be fun," Kristy replied, "but you need lots and lots of lemons to make enough lemonade for eight people. I'm sure we've only got two or three. We hardly ever use them."

"Darn," said Karen.

"*I've* got plenty of lemons," spoke up a hoarse voice. "You children come on over here and I'll show you how to make real lemonade."

Eight heads swiveled slowly in the direction of the Halloween house. There stood Mrs. Porter, frizzy gray hair, frumpy black clothes, and all.

Kristy thought it was to the kids' credit that not one of them screamed, but she realized later that they were simply frozen with horror.

"Please?" croaked Mrs. Porter. "I hardly ever have guests."

Kristy looked from the terrified children to Mrs. Porter. She couldn't help but remember the time she'd been baby-sitting and Mrs. Porter had brought over the remains of a mouse, saying that Boo-Boo had killed it and left the insides on her front porch. On the other hand, Mrs. Porter had also brought over a wedding present when Kristy's mom and Watson had gotten married. Kristy kept thinking about what Mrs. Porter had just said: "I hardly ever have guests." She began to feel sorry for her. So she made one of the snap decisions she's famous for. "Come on, you guys. What fun! Real lemonade! Thanks, Mrs. Porter."

Mrs. Porter's mouth cracked into a crooked smile. "How lovely. Guests," she said. "Come over in five minutes and I'll have everything ready. Heh, heh, heh." She whisked around, her robes swinging out behind her, and dashed toward her house.

"Kris-teee," Karen wailed softly. "You're not making us go over there, are you?"

"We are all going over. We'll have some nice lemonade," Kristy replied, putting Shannon and Boo-Boo in the house.

"Not me," said Amanda, following Kristy. "Max and I are going home. You're not the boss of us."

"That's true," said Kristy. "And I'm sure the other kids won't think you two are 'fraidy cats if you go home now."

"We *aren't* 'fraidy cats!" cried Max.

"Right," said Kristy.

"Well, we aren't!"

"Neither . . . neither are we," spoke up Karen, apparently meaning herself, Andrew, David Michael, Linny, and Hannie.

"Of course not. I didn't say you were. Now — I'm ready to go to Mrs. Porter's. Who's coming with me?" asked Kristy.

Reluctantly, all of the kids followed her to Mrs. Porter's porch. They waited nervously on the front steps, and in a minute she appeared with a pitcher of lemonade and a stack of paper cups.

"Here we go," she said, and began to pour. She also began to cackle. Karen looked ready to faint, but Mrs. Porter gave a tiny smile. (Kristy almost thought she saw Mrs. Porter wink.)

"I thought you were going to show us how to make this," said Karen warily. She gazed around the sagging front porch.

"Was I?" said Mrs. Porter. "Well, I brewed it up pretty quickly." She reached into the house and pulled a broom onto the front porch.

When Karen's eyes fell on a broom, Kristy thought Karen was going to faint. But Karen drew in a deep breath and remained upright.

"What, um, what's in this . . . brew?" asked Linny. "I mean, how *do* you make lemonade?" He was eyeing the broom, too.

"You just squeeze some fresh lemons . . ." Mrs. Porter started to explain.

Kristy lost track of the explanation. She was watching Mrs. Porter fill the cups. When she finished, she handed one to everybody, including Kristy. No one took a sip, though. They all just stared nervously into the cups.

"Go ahead. Drink up," said Mrs. Porter. "It won't kill you."

"Are you sure?" whispered Karen.

Kristy knew she would have to be first. She brought the cup to her mouth, trying to sniff the lemonade before she swallowed any of it. All she smelled was lemons, but she was still wary. Then she glanced at Mrs. Porter, who was looking back at Kristy. Kristy dared to open her mouth.

"Hey! This is great, Mrs. Porter!" she exclaimed honestly after she'd taken a swallow.

"It *is*?" asked Max, Andrew, and David Michael.

"The best ever."

Cautiously, the others sipped their lemonade.

"It *is* good," Karen agreed, but Kristy knew she was just waiting for one of them to go up in smoke, sprout stringy black hair, and turn into a witch.

Ten minutes later, the kids were still fine.

Mrs. Porter was seated in a wicker chair, watching them. Her broom was leaning against the chair and a black cat was asleep in her lap. "Heh, heh, heh," cackled Mrs. Porter.

"Kristy!" Andrew was tugging at Kristy's hand. "I have to go to the bathroom."

"See that? He's sick," Karen whispered urgently.

"No, I'm not," Andrew replied indignantly. "I just have to go. Now."

Kristy knew what "now" meant to Andrew. "Mrs. Porter," she began, "I'm really sorry, but could we use your bathroom?"

"Of course," croaked Mrs. Porter. "Down the hall, past the kitchen, first door on the left."

Kristy held the front door open for Andrew and followed him inside. Karen slipped in behind them. "*I'm* not staying out there with *her*," she whispered.

David Michael followed. "Neither am I," he said.

"Me neither," said Hannie, Linny, Amanda, and Max.

Kristy sighed.

The kids crept through a hallway in single file. The house was dark and dreary and musty-smelling, but somehow, Kristy decided, not actually spooky. Just old, and a little lonely.

Karen didn't agree. She shivered. "I feel ghosts," she announced. "Ghosts and witches."

Kristy rolled her eyes.

It was after Andrew had used the bathroom and the kids were passing the kitchen for the second time that Kristy noticed the two empty cans of frozen lemonade on the counter. She didn't point them out, though, and she didn't say anything to Mrs. Porter. But she thought she now knew a secret about her neighbor. Old Mrs. Porter was just a lonely woman who wanted company.

Of course, Kristy thought as she returned to the front porch and looked at Mrs. Porter, the black cat, and the broomstick, you could never be sure.

CHAPTER 10

I felt awful. My heart was racing and my mouth was dry.

I wasn't sick; I was just plain nervous. I was on my way over to Charlotte Johanssen's to baby-sit, and I had decided it was time to tell her that I was moving.

With a sweaty hand I held my Kid-Kit. Kristy dreamed up Kid-Kits not long after we started the Baby-sitters Club. Kid-Kits are boxes (each of us sitters has one) that we decorated and keep filled with our old games and toys and books, and usually a few new coloring books and activity books paid for out of club dues. We bring our Kid-Kits along sometimes when we baby-sit. The kids love them, therefore they like us, therefore their parents like us, and therefore Kid-Kits are good for business. Charlotte has always been a big fan of Kid-Kits, and especially of the books inside. She loves to read.

So. I had one sweaty hand and one shaking hand. The shaking hand was shaking because it was time to ring the Johanssens' doorbell. I raised my hand and imagined that the ding-dong was going to sound shaky, too. Like this: D**{**NG-**D**O**N**G. But of course it sounded just fine.

Charlotte was at the door in a flash. "Hi, Stacey! Hi, Stacey! I got three gold stars in school today! I have twenty-one altogether. And when you have twenty-five you get to be the teacher's helper for one whole day!"

"That's wonderful, Charlotte!" I exclaimed. "I'm really proud of you!"

"Thanks. Boy, remember last year when I hated school? Now it's the funnest thing ever. And guess who my best friend is."

"Mmm, I give up."

"Valerie Namm. Valerie is the most popular girl in the whole fourth grade. And I'm really just eight. I'm only supposed to be in *third* grade, so —"

"Charlotte, excuse me, honey," said her mother from behind her. "Let Stacey inside. And let me speak to her for just a minute, okay? Then you two can talk all afternoon."

"Okay," said Charlotte reluctantly.

"Why don't you go upstairs and find the planet chart you made," suggested Dr.

Johannsen. "I think Stacey would like to see it."

"Okay," said Charlotte again, and ran up to her room.

"Stacey," Dr. Johanssen said, at the same time I said, "Dr. Johanssen."

We laughed. "Go ahead," I told her.

"Well." Dr. Johanssen looked uncomfortable, as if she had something to say, but didn't want to say it. She cleared her throat. "I heard a rumor today," she finally began. "I heard that your family is moving. And then I drove by your house and saw the for-sale sign."

I sighed. "That was what I wanted to talk to you about. We *are* moving. I was going to tell Charlotte everything today. If that's okay with you."

"Oh, it's fine, Stacey. Thank you. You're so responsible. And, boy, are we going to miss you."

"Believe me, I'm going to miss you, too," I said.

Dr. Johanssen reached out to give me a hug, but we heard Charlotte's footsteps on the stairs then, so she gave me a quick kiss on the cheek instead. "Good luck," she whispered. Then she raised her voice. " 'Bye, Char. I'm going to the hospital now. Daddy will be home at six."

"Okay! 'Bye, Mom!" Charlotte jumped down the last step.

"I couldn't find the planet chart." She dove for the Kid-Kit. "What's in it today, Stacey?" she asked as she carried it into the living room. This was our ritual. We always opened the Kid-Kit on the floor in the living room, Charlotte taking the things out slowly so she could examine each one.

"Some of the same stuff and a few new things, including a new book," I replied.

"A new book? Oh, goody. We need one now that we're done with *The Borrowers*." Charlotte emptied the Kid-Kit and, just as I'd hoped, put everything aside except the one book she hadn't seen before. It was called *Iggy's House*, by Judy Blume. "*Iggy's House*. That's a funny title," said Charlotte. "What's it about?"

"Well," I said carefully, "it's about a family that moves away."

Charlotte looked thoughtful. "The last time I moved I was two. I don't remember it at all."

"The last time I moved was when I moved here. That was just one year ago. A year and a couple of months."

"I'm glad you moved here," said Charlotte, settling herself in my lap, and opening *Iggy* to the first page.

"Me, too. But . . ." (I couldn't put it off any longer) "I have to tell you something, Charlotte. We're moving again."

Charlotte wrenched her neck around and peered at me. "What?"

"We're moving back to New York in a couple of weeks."

"You mean you're leaving Stoneybrook? You're leaving *me*?"

I nodded. I watched Charlotte take in the awful information. She looked like she had just swallowed horrible medicine.

Iggy's House slipped to the floor as Charlotte put her head in her hands and began to cry.

"I'm really sorry, Char," I said. "I don't want to go. But my dad's job is changing. We *have* to move." I wrapped my arms around Charlotte, and she let me hold her for several moments. Then suddenly she leaped up and started shouting. "I hate you!" she cried. "I hate you! You're mean! I thought you liked baby-sitting for me."

"I do. I love it," I told her. "That doesn't have anything to do with the move. It's my dad's job, just like I told you. I wish I could stay in Stoneybrook, too."

For a moment I thought Charlotte was going to turn around and run upstairs to her room. Instead, she slowly crossed the room back to me. When I stood up she put her arms around my waist in a desperate hug.

I had an idea. "Would you like to come over to my house?" I asked Charlotte. I thought it might help her to understand things. It wouldn't help explain *why* we were moving, but I decided it would be better if the move were gradual. Seeing our house while it was being packed up might be easier on her than just "here today, gone tomorrow."

"Okay," Charlotte replied, drying her eyes. "But why?"

"I'll show you what's going on over there. You might think it's interesting. We have to pack up every single thing in the house."

"Where will you find enough boxes?"

"The moving company gives us cartons. You'll see. Some of them are full of stuff already. Come on. Let's go."

I wrote a short note to Dr. Johanssen and then Charlotte and I walked hand-in-hand over to my house. Charlotte doesn't know any kids on my street, so she rarely comes to my part of the neighborhood, which was why she hadn't seen the for-sale sign in our yard before.

"Your house still looks the same," Charlotte said as we approached it.

"From the outside, yes. Wait'll we get inside."

I opened the front door. We were greeted by the sight of my mother's backside. It was sticking out of a closet in the hallway. On the floor outside the closet was a heap of boots and shoes and gloves, a tennis racket, some tennis balls, a yardstick, a deflated football (who had that belonged to? Dad?), and a stepladder. As we approached my mother, she tossed an ancient pair of ballet slippers onto the pile.

"Ahem," I said. "Hi, Mom."

My mother jumped a mile, then straightened up, hitting her head on the coat hangers.

"Stacey! You startled me!"

"Sorry," I said sheepishly. "Mom, I brought Charlotte over to show her the progress we're making."

"Oh, hi, honey," my mother said to Charlotte. "Have you ever seen such a mess?"

Charlotte shook her head shyly.

"Come on, Char," I said, taking her hand. "I'll show you my room first."

My room was a good place to start because not much had been done to it. I'd cleaned out a lot of stuff for the yard sale, and put some of my books into boxes, but that was about all.

"This doesn't look too different," said Charlotte.

"I know. Mom's frantic. She keeps telling me to 'get cracking.' Look at my parents' room."

I led Charlotte into Mom and Dad's bedroom. The walls were bare. The tops of their dressers were bare. Their bookshelves were empty. Packing cartons and paper cluttered all of the floor space.

"Whoa," said Charlotte, looking at the cartons. "I hope you're moving to another big house."

"We're not," I replied. I told her about the apartment. Then I told her about the yard sale.

"A yard sale!" Charlotte exclaimed, brightening, "I *love* yard sales. We got my dresser at the Berks' sale. It only cost seven dollars. And I got a Barbie doll and a dollhouse at a yard sale in Sheridan, and you know how much both of them cost? Just two dollars. Two dollars *all together*. My dad said, 'Cheap at twice the price.' "

I laughed. "Come on down to the basement. You can see how we're getting ready for our yard sale. If there's something you want, I'll set it aside for you."

Charlotte was really perking up. She ran ahead of me all the way down to the basement. If I'd known she liked yard sales so much, I would have told her about ours before I told her about the move.

"Kristy and Claudia and Dawn and Mary Anne and I are going to run the sale," I explained to Charlotte when we reached the basement. "See? We're tagging everything and writing down the prices. We're making ads, too. In a couple of days we're going to tape them up on all the trees around here. And in other parts of town, too."

"This sure is a lot of stuff," said Charlotte, awed. She began poking through a pile of clothes. Then she saw a stack of my old games. "Oh, Boggle!" she cried. "And Operation!" Her eyes lit on a doll and then on a copy of *The Cricket in Times Square.* Ordinarily, I don't give my books away, especially not hardcovers, but someone had given me a second copy of *The Cricket.* It looked almost new. Kristy had priced it at fifty cents.

"Remember when we read this together?" asked Charlotte.

"Sure I do. That was fun."

"Save it for me, okay? That's what I want you to put aside."

"I'll do better than that," I told her. I peeled the price tag off the book. Then I found a pen, opened the cover, and inside wrote "Love to

Charlotte, my favorite kid, from Stacey, her favorite baby-sitter."

I handed the book to Charlotte. "This is for you," I told her. "To remember me by."

Charlotte took the book and looked at the cover fondly for a long time. Then she burst into tears.

CHAPTER 11

This afternoon, Buddy and Suzi Barrett learned a business lesson. Unfortunately, it was sort of a hard lesson, but in the end everything worked out okay. Better than okay, even. (I wish I could be more specific right now, but I can't.)

The reason Dawn couldn't be more specific was that I would read the diary, and Dawn had had an idea for my party, which, of course, she didn't want me to find out about.

Anyway, Buddy and Suzi had come up with what they thought was a great way to earn some money. They'd gotten the idea when they saw the ads for Stacey's yard sale. The thing was, busy

Mrs. Barrett didn't want to be around when Buddy and Suzi put their plan into action. She left the project for when I was baby-sitting. (She did pay me extra for my trouble, though.)

This is what happened with the Barretts and poor Dawn. It started when Mrs. Barrett asked her two older kids, eight-year-old Buddy and five-year-old Suzi, to clean their rooms. Not just to clean them *up*, but to clean them *out*. Of course, this caused hysteria. No kid likes to clean anything up or out, especially a bedroom. But then Buddy saw the signs for our yard sale and got an idea. He asked his mother if he and Suzi could sell the junk they didn't want, instead of just throwing it out. Mrs. Barrett decided that was all right with her, but asked the kids if they could wait until Thursday afternoon to hold their sale. That was when Mrs. Barrett would be at work. (Mr. and Mrs. Barrett are divorced, and Mrs. Barrett has a part-time job). It was also the day Dawn would be baby-sitting.

It was just like Mrs. Barrett not to mention this to Dawn beforehand. Mrs. Barrett is nice but too busy. She's always forgetting to tell us baby-sitters important things. (I will say, though, that she's much, much more responsible than she used to be. At least, after she sprang this surprise project on Dawn she told her she'd pay her fifty cents per hour extra for her trouble.)

Dawn had to be at the Barretts' house *right* after school that day in order for Mrs. Barrett to get to her job on time. When she was let inside, she was greeted by an exuberant Buddy and Suzi, a mountain of old toys in the living room, Marnie Barrett (who's only two) squawking in her high chair, Pow (the Barretts' bassett hound) making a mess with dog kibble on the kitchen floor, and Mrs. Barrett dashing for the back door, calling over her shoulder, "You know where the phone numbers are, Dawn. Oh, by the way, I told Buddy and Suzi they could hold a sidewalk sale today. Back at six! 'Bye, kids!"

"Wait a sec!" Dawn cried, chasing after Mrs. Barrett. "What are they selling?"

"All the stuff on the living room floor!" Mrs. Barrett closed the door to the garage after her.

Dawn opened it again. "Is the stuff priced?" she asked.

"No. You can help them with that." Mrs. Barrett climbed into her car.

Dawn ran to the window and knocked on

it. "What are we going to set up the stuff on?"

"Oh. There's a card table in the closet in the front hall." She started the car.

"What shall I do with Marnie?" Dawn shouted.

"Put her in the playpen. It's folded up in the rec room. Have fun!"

Mrs. Barrett backed out of the garage.

"Oh, brother," Dawn said under her breath. She ran back to the living room. Buddy and Suzi were nearly hysterical with excitement.

"It's sidewalk sale day! It's sidewalk sale day!" they kept shouting as they jumped around their pile of toys.

"Let's get started, Dawn!" cried Buddy.

"Wait a sec," said Dawn "Just a minute. Okay?" She put Pow's kibble away and sent Pow outside. Then she lifted Marnie out of her high chair. "Poor Marnie-o," she said. "You're wet. And I bet you'd like to play outside, wouldn't you?"

"No-no," replied Marnie, but she was smiling. She answers every question with no-no.

Dawn changed Marnie and put her playpen in the front yard near the sidewalk. Then she helped Buddy and Suzi set up the card table and lug all their stuff out to it. At last she plopped Marnie in the playpen with a few toys and a graham cracker.

"Okay, guys," she said to Buddy and Suzi. "I guess you're in business." But she knew their sale was doomed from the start.

"What do we do first?" Suzi wondered.

"I think you should sort of arrange the stuff on the table," replied Dawn. "You know, fix it up so it looks like a real store, all nice and neat, and like you'd want to buy something. And arrange it so people can find what they're looking for. Put all the games in one pile, all the trucks together, that sort of thing."

The Barretts busied themselves with their wares while Dawn played "Where is Thumbkin?" with Marnie.

"Okay," Suzi said a few minutes later. "All finished. Where are our customers?"

They watched a few cars drive by.

"You need a sign, I think," said Dawn.

So Buddy made a sign on a piece of construction paper that read:

TOY SALE
COME ONE, COME ALL

He hung it on the front of the table.

A few more cars drove by. One of them slowed down so the driver could read the sign, but then it sped up and went on.

"Try shouting," suggested Dawn.

The next time a car approached Buddy yelled, "Toy sale! Toy sale! Buy our toys!"

Suzi yelled, "Hey, slow down! Stop! . . . STOP!"

The driver smiled and waved but didn't stop.

"I think the problem is that no one knew about the sale ahead of time," said Dawn.

"We told the Pikes about it," Buddy informed her. And at that moment, three of the Pike kids showed up.

"You want to buy something?" asked Suzi hopefully, hopping from one foot to the other.

"Sure," replied Vanessa Pike. "I've got fifty cents."

"We don't have any money," said Claire, speaking for herself and Margo. "We just want to look."

The Pikes looked over the toy selection. Finally, Vanessa said, "I think I'd like to buy that tow truck. I could give it to Nicky for his birthday. How much is it?"

"Two dollars," said Buddy.

"Five cents," said Suzi.

"*How* much?" asked Vanessa.

The Barretts shrugged. They turned to Dawn for help.

"I think you should charge ten cents," Dawn

told them. (She'd had a lot of experience pricing things lately.)

"Ten cents?!" cried Buddy.

"It's used," Dawn pointed out. "And it's just a little truck."

The ten-cent truck was the only sale the Barretts made that afternoon. By five o'clock, they were bored and disappointed, and Dawn thought they ought to close up shop. When the last of their toys had been carried back inside, Dawn decided to tell Buddy and Suzi how our yard sale was being organized. She didn't want to sound like an I-told-you-so person, but she thought it might help them to know about the benefits of advertising and planning ahead. Then she even told them that they could set up a booth at my yard sale.

The Barretts were ecstatic, but it turned out that they were actually more interested in the fact that I was moving than in the sale.

"Will you miss Stacey?" Buddy asked Dawn.

"I sure will," she replied. "All her friends will. We're going to give her a big party before she leaves."

"A party! Can we come?" asked Suzi.

It was that simple question — Can we come? — that gave Dawn the idea my friends had been looking for. Suddenly, Dawn knew just what kind of party to throw me. When she left the Barretts' that evening, she ran home and phoned Kristy right away.

"I've got it!" she cried. "I thought of a special, meaningful, *wonderful* party for Stacey."

"Thank goodness," said Kristy. "I was really getting worried. Tell me!"

"Well, it involves children," Dawn began, and then she explained her idea.

"Fabulous!" Kristy exclaimed when Dawn was finished. "I'll call Mary Anne, you call Claudia. Then the four of us better get together without Stacey sometime *soon*. Maybe tomorrow before the club meeting."

"Perfect," said Dawn. She was smiling when she hung up the phone, and she knew Kristy was, too.

CHAPTER 12

On Saturday morning I woke up with butterflies in my stomach. I'm not sure how it's possible to feel nervous while you're *asleep*, but that must have been what was happening, because when I opened my eyes, the butterflies were already there.

It was yard sale day.

I jumped out of bed excitedly. I could see, even without raising the shade, that the sun was shining. My friends and I would just have died if it had been raining and we'd actually had to hold the sale on the rain date.

It was 7:30. The sale was to be held from 10:00 until 4:30. Claudia, Kristy, Mary Anne, and Dawn were going to come over at 8:30 to set everything up. For an hour I raced around the house, getting dressed, eating breakfast, checking on a million things. My parents thought I was going to give myself a heart attack.

"Relax, slow down," said Dad.

"But I just realized something! We don't have any change to start off with! What if the very first customer pays for a fifty-cent toy with a five-dollar bill?"

"Relax. I'll give you ten dollars in change," my father told me. "You can pay me back when the sale's over."

"Oh, thanks!" I cried, and ran down to the basement to look at our junk.

My friends showed up right on time. They were as excited as I was. Mary Anne was wringing her hands. "We only have an hour and a half!" she wailed.

"Cut it out," said Dawn, who was twisting her hair nervously. "I feel like a wind-up toy that someone wound up too tight."

"Okay, you guys. Relax, slow down," I said, echoing my father's words. "Let's get to work."

Everyone drew in deep breaths and let them out slowly.

"All right," said Kristy. "Where'd you put the folding tables?"

The night before, my friends had brought over a ton of stuff from their own houses: four long folding tables for us to set the sale items on; some folding chairs; a stack of signs that read Jewelry, Toys, Books, Clothes, etc.; several boxes of Claudia's Heavenly Brownies; several flats of Dawn's baby spider plants;

some of Mary Anne's handmade goodies (felt eyeglass cases, knitted scarves and belts, and potholders); and lemonade and limeade mix. Then Buddy and Suzi Barrett had brought their toys over. They were going to try to sell them again.

"The folding tables are in the garage," I replied.

"All right," said Kristy, "let's set them up."

She was taking charge as usual, and I let her because I figured she knew a lot more about yard sales than I did.

My friends and I arranged the four tables, plus two of our own in the garage, spilling out onto the driveway. We set the chairs behind the tables.

"Now for the sale stuff," said Kristy. "Let's haul the things out of the basement first, and then worry about the plants and the food."

Armload by armload we carried my junk out of the basement. We arranged it until the tables looked more like displays in Bellair's Department Store than just old tables in our dusty garage. When everything was neat and the signs were in place, my dad helped us fold up the Ping-Pong table and carry that out of the basement. We set it on the driveway.

"I guess the other big items should go on the driveway, too," I said. (The other big items

were a vacuum cleaner, a desk-top Xerox machine my father had never used, all of our
gardening tools, a huge fan, some window
boxes, a weeping fig tree in a wooden tub,
and a statue my mother had brought for our
garden.)

When that was done, I looked at my watch.
"Nine-thirty-five!" I screeched. "People will be
here in twenty-five minutes! The lemonade's
not mixed. Or the limeade. Claudia, you have
to cut the brownies into squares! Where are
the napkins? And who's going to be in charge
of selling what?"

With some help from my mother, we got
everything mixed, cut up, found, and figured
out by 9:50. The Barretts even arrived and set
up *their* table. Not a moment too soon. Mrs.
Prezzioso and her bratty daughter Jenny showed
up then.

"Hi!" Mrs. P. called gaily. "I hope you don't
mind that we're early. We always like to get
to sales first so we can have the pick of the
litter, if you know what I mean."

I did, sort of.

Kristy, who was manning the table with the
toys and books, turned to me excitedly. "I just
love selling things," she exclaimed. "And making money. This is going to be a great day!"

(Kristy doesn't *need* much money, thanks to wealthy Watson; she simply has a talent for making money, and she likes being a businesswoman. I guess she takes after her mom. Kristy's mother is really smart.)

Jenny trailed her mother around from table to table and finally paused in front of Kristy's to look at the toys. Mrs. P. paused in front of the statue. "Lovely," she murmured. "A real find."

Next to arrive were the entire Newton family and Mr. Spier, Mary Anne's father. Before I knew it, Mr. Marshall was walking up our driveway with Nina and Eleanor, followed by the Perkinses. Mrs. Perkins looked so pregnant, I began to wonder what would happen if she started having labor pains right in our garage.

Then the questions began flying.

"How old is the Xerox machine?" Mr. Marshall wanted to know.

(I had to find my father in order to answer him.)

"Is this statue made of marble?" asked Mrs. P.

"No, just fancy cement," I replied.

"Would you say the Ping-Pong table is in good condition?" asked Mr. Perkins.

"Definitely," I answered. "It's only six months old and we didn't use it that much."

"Mommy, can I have this dolly?" Jenny asked. (At last — a question that wasn't for me.)

Mrs. Prezzioso glanced up in distaste. "That ratty old thing?" she said, and I bristled. "That ratty old thing" was Amelia Jane and she was ten years old and I used to love her. I considered telling Mrs. P. she wasn't for sale after all, that she'd gotten in by mistake.

But before I could say a word, a woman I didn't know waddled over to Dawn and said, "Are the shutters for sale?"

Dawn glanced at me with raised eyebrows. "What shutters?" she asked.

"The ones on the front of the house."

I choked back a laugh. I wanted to say, "Are you out of your mind?" Instead I just shook my head slightly at Dawn.

Dawn answered the woman in a professional, adult voice. "No, I'm sorry. They're not."

"I'll give you seventy-five dollars for them."

"Seventy-five dollars!" Dawn couldn't help exclaiming.

I cleared my throat. "I'll check with my father," I said.

"No, they're not," Dad spoke up. He was

standing in the doorway to the garage and had heard everything.

Dawn and I shrugged. "Sorry," we told the woman.

She bought a three-dollar sweater for her daughter and left.

I heard screams coming from near Kristy.

"Mommy, I *want* that *dolly!*" It was Jenny.

"All *right* . . . my little angel." Mrs P. gave in. "But then we're going home."

Good, I thought.

Mrs. P. paid for the statue and Amelia Jane, and led Jenny away.

I looked around. The sale had been on for about a half hour and it was really jumping. People were milling around, looking at the tables and the things in the driveway. Claudia was serving up drinks and brownies. Two spider plants had sold, as well as a couple of Mary Anne's handicraft projects. Mary Anne was beaming. And the Barretts had sold several of their toys. They looked very excited.

All five of us club members were running back and forth, answering questions and borrowing change from each other's cash boxes.

Five of the Pikes arrived. The Perkinses left with the Ping-Pong table. "Thank you, Daddy!" Myriah and Gabbie were singing.

Mr. Marshall was looking at the walls of the

garage. They were totally bare except for this length of dirty old rope, which was hanging from a peg.

Suddenly, Mr. Marshall grabbed the rope from the wall. "How much is this?" he asked Dawn.

"Well, it isn't really for s —"

"I'll give you fifty cents for it."

The rope was just something we hadn't bothered to throw out. It was worth exactly zero cents.

"It's a sale!" I called to Dawn.

The day flew by. Logan Bruno (one of our associate club members) and Trevor Sandbourne (an old boyfriend of Claudia's) arrived. Then Howie Johnson and Dori Wallingford (the King and Queen Rat) showed up. I refused to look at them. Instead, I looked in our cash boxes. They were stuffed! And our tables were growing empty. The brownies and spider plants were long gone.

Howie wanted to buy a turquoise ring (that used to be mine) to give to Dori. I made him pay Mary Anne.

At 4:00, it occurred to me that Charlotte hadn't come over. But I got distracted by a man smoking a cigar who wanted to know how much we were selling our car for.

"We can't sell it," I told him. "We need it."

He gave me a disgusted look and left.

Some people have absolutely no idea about how yard sales work.

"Stacey?" said a small voice.

I turned around. "Charlotte! I'm glad you came!" I hugged her.

"Stacey," she said again. "You know I love yard sales."

I nodded.

"But I just didn't want to come after all. I didn't want to see you selling your things. That's why I'm late. And I don't want to buy anything. I want to give you this." Charlotte shoved a package into my hands and ran down the driveway.

Even though a bunch of people were still milling around, I opened the package. It was wrapped in Snoopy paper. Inside was a little book that Charlotte had made herself. The story was called "The Girl Who Moved Away." And the first page said, "Dedication: This book is for my favorite baby-sitter from her favorite kid. To remember me by."

I would have started crying right there in the middle of everything if another man hadn't approached me wanting to know how much the folding tables were.

I told him they were six hundred dollars.

It was time to close up shop.

By dinnertime, our garage looked like a garage again. Everything was put away. The stuff we hadn't sold was in a carton for Goodwill. (There wasn't much in the carton.) The Barretts had left, happy with the money they had earned. Now my friends and I were doing the fun part. We were totaling up the money in the cash boxes. When I announced the final figure, Kristy pretended to faint.

"We're practically millionaires!" she cried as she crashed to the ground.

I had to agree. Even split up, and even after we'd paid my father back the ten dollars he'd lent us, each share was a lot more money than I'd seen in a long time.

My friends looked like they had dollar signs for pupils. They were unusually excited. I mean, this was a lot of money, but what was going on? Of course, I didn't know it then, but what they were thinking was that my party was definitely going to be one MAJOR celebration.

CHAPTER 13

I just love parties. So when I got an invitation to one a couple of days after the yard sale, I was thrilled. It was from the other members of the club, and it instructed me to come to a farewell party in my honor at Kristy's house at two o'clock the following Saturday.

Although I was excited (and touched), I thought that a number of things about the invitation were strange. For starters, my friends and I almost never send written invitations to parties anymore. We just pick up the phone and say, "Come to a party." Sometimes we don't even do that. We go around school inviting anyone we see. For another thing, two o'clock in the afternoon was a funny time for a party. Most of our parties are held on Friday or Saturday evening. A third thing — the invitation said: *Important! Wear old clothes!* What were we going to do? Paint Kristy's room?

When I called Kristy to tell her that of course I'd be at my party, I asked her about the old clothes and stuff, but she wouldn't say a word. Something was up. I just knew it.

On Saturday, I pulled on a pair of blue stretch pants and a white sweat shirt decorated with stars and sequins.

Kristy called me at one o'clock. "What are you wearing?" she asked.

I told her.

"Much too nice," she replied. "Put on jeans and your gray sweat shirt — if they're not packed."

"*Those* rags?"

"Are they packed yet?"

"No."

"Then trust me. Put them on."

When Dad dropped me off at Kristy's an hour later, I was wearing the jeans and the sweat shirt. I looked like I was ready to do yard work. Or paint a room.

I rang the bell next to the massive front door of Watson Brewer's mansion. When Kristy answered, I waved to my father and he drove off. Kristy was wearing jeans and a blue sweat shirt.

"At least I'm not underdressed," I kidded her.

She smiled and led me through the house

and to the back door. "Now close your eyes," she said as she turned the knob.

I wondered why I needed to do that since I knew who was going to be in the yard — Claudia, Mary Anne, Dawn, Logan Bruno and Shannon Kilbourne (associate club members), Pete Black, Rick Chow, maybe Trevor Sandbourne, and Emily Bernstein. I hoped Howie Johnson and Dori Wallingford hadn't been invited, but I figured Claudia would know better.

Kristy flung the door open.

"SURPRISE!" shouted a loud chorus of voices.

My jaw dropped practically to my knees.

The guests were not who I had expected at all. Claudia, Mary Anne, Dawn, Logan, and Shannon were there, but the other guests were *children* . . . all the kids (except for babies) that our club sits for. As I looked slowly around at the grinning faces, I saw the eight Pikes — Mallory, Byron, Jordan, Adam, Vanessa, Nicky, Margo, and Claire; Jamie Newton; Myriah and Gabbie Perkins; Charlotte Johanssen; Buddy and Suzi Barrett; Dawn's brother, Jeff; Kristy's brother, David Michael; Karen and Andrew; Nina and Eleanor Marshall; Jackie, Shea, and Archie Rodowsky; Hannie and Linny Papadakis; Amanda and Max Delaney; and even Jenny Prezzioso. (I guess they really couldn't leave her out.) The yard was twinkling with tiny golden lights, and lanterns and bunches of balloons were strung up everywhere.

"Oh, wow!" I said softly.

"Did we surprise you? Did we surprise you?" cried Karen, jumping up and down.

"You sure did."

Charlotte stepped forward and handed me a little corsage made of chrysanthemums. Kristy helped her pin it to my sweat shirt.

"These flowers are for you," Charlotte said, obviously reciting something she'd memorized. "Today is your special day. We are all here to honor you, to say good-bye, and to . . ." (She turned to the other children.)

"HAVE FUN!" they shouted.

I wondered if I was supposed to say something, but Kristy spoke up then. "This is a party not just for Stacey, but for everybody here," she said. "And everyone is going to have a good time. I guarantee it. So . . . let the fun begin!"

"What are we going to do first?" asked Karen.

"We're going to have an egg relay race," Kristy replied.

I couldn't imagine how my friends were going to organize twenty-eight children into a relay race, but they did — and fast, too. They were all prepared. They'd carefully figured out five teams (uneven in numbers, but even in ability), and they handed out eggs and spoons in the wink of an eye.

Soon, little kids were charging back and forth across the yard with fragile eggs balanced on spoons. Jenny tripped and her egg splattered to the ground. Her teammates moaned. They were out of the race.

Then Buddy Barrett and David Michael crashed into each other and squashed their eggs on their fronts.

"I see why we were supposed to wear old clothes," I whispered to Mary Anne, and she grinned.

Only two teams were left, and it looked as if the race might end in a tie. Myriah Perkins and Jamie Newton were both heading for the finish at the same pace. But just a few steps from the end, Jamie's egg seemed to fly off the spoon all by itself. *Squish*.

"I won! I won!" Myriah shouted as she and her egg made it safely back home.

"You mean, we *all* won," said Karen, who was her teammate.

"Congratulations," said Claudia. "Prizes for everyone on Myriah's team." And she handed each child a Silly Putty egg. The prizes came from a big box. I peeked inside. It was chock full of toys!

"Where'd you get the money for all this?" I asked incredulously. "I don't mean to be rude, but . . ."

"Where do you think?" answered Dawn with a smile. "From the yard sale. Thanks to your junk, we are going to have one hot party!"

"Oh, no!" I cried, giggling. "I don't believe it. You guys spent that money on this party?"

"Every last cent."

"You're too much," I said tearfully.

I was about to turn on the waterworks, but luckily Kristy announced that it was time for some more fun. And she wasn't kidding. During the next hour or so, us baby-sitters held our own egg race, the kids played Musical Rug (easier than Musical Chairs when a lot of children are involved) and Pin-the-Baby-on-the-Sitter (for that game, Claudia had drawn a picture of me holding out my arms, and made twenty-eight crying babies that were supposed to go *in* my arms). The children hunted for peanuts and ran races, and we all played Simon Says. The winner, or winners, of each game received a pretty nice prize — a Transformer, a sticker book, a Slinky, a bag of Gummi Bears.

By the time Simon Says was over and Jordan Pike had been given a Transformer, half the kids were getting tired, and the other half were hysterical with excitement.

"Time to quiet down," Kristy whispered to the rest of us club members. "Mary Anne, can you help me? And Dawn and Stacey, can you get all the kids to the front of the house? Keep them right by the driveway."

We followed Kristy's instructions. I was beginning to feel like a teacher. I decided it was a nice feeling.

When the kids were standing quietly along the drive, Kristy and Mary Anne unrolled a long sheet of brown paper and handed out crayons.

"What's this for?" asked Gabbie Perkins, looking uncertainly at the paper.

"Well," Claudia replied, "Stacey's moving to New York, but we don't want her to forget Stoneybrook, do we?"

"No!" cried the kids.

"So we're going to draw her a big picture of our town. You can put in your streets and your houses and yourselves. Then Stacey will always remember us."

The kids set to work right away. The next fifteen minutes were filled with giggles and shouts and calls of, "I don't have green hair!"

and, "Hey, your house goes here, not there," and, "What did you draw a pond for? There's no pond in our yard!"

I have to admit that when the kids got tired of drawing, the mural looked nothing like Stoneybrook, but it didn't matter. It was a great picture. Kristy made a big deal out of rolling it up, tying it with a red ribbon, and having Hannie Papadakis present it to me. I knew I would keep it forever.

"And now," said Kristy, loving every second of being in charge, "back to the yard. And Charlotte, you blindfold Stacey, okay?"

Charlotte nodded importantly.

When we were gathered in the yard again and my eyes were bound so tightly that I couldn't even see the daylight, a hush fell over the party.

Then I heard singing. Twenty-eight little voices and six bigger voices were joined together singing a song to the tune of "Happy Birthday": "Farewe-ell to you, Farewe-ell to you. Farewe-ell, dear Stacey. Farewell and good luck!"

The blindfold was removed. As if by magic, a table had appeared, and on it were paper plates, napkins, cups, a pitcher of punch, and two cakes. One was a huge sheet cake decorated with pink flowers. In blue frosting was written: GOOD-BYE STACEY, GOOD-BYE. The other cake was tiny and said simply: STACEY.

"The little one's for you," Claudia whispered to me. "The bakery makes a special no-sugar cake for people with diabetes. The other cake is for the rest of us."

"That's so sweet," I said, giving her a hug, and adding, "No pun intended. Seriously. You guys thought of everything. I really appreciate it."

So I ate my little cake and the kids and my friends gobbled up the big cake. Then Mary Anne found an excuse to award a prize to any kid who hadn't already won one (most original picture on the mural, neatest cake-eater, that sort of thing).

A few minutes later the parents started arriving to pick up their crayon-y, egg-smeared, cake-covered children. As each guest left the party, instead of receiving a "goody bag," he or she handed *me* a homemade card. Kristy had asked them to make the cards the previous week and bring them to the party.

I read all the cards many times that night. The funniest was Margo Pike's, which said: GOOD LICK STASY. HAVE FUN IN NEW YURK. The one that made me cry was Charlotte's (of course): GOOD-BYE, STACEY. I WILL ALWAYS MISS YOU. I WISH YOU WERE MY SISTER.

Well, I would always miss Charlotte and the other children and my Stoneybrook friends. I would never, ever forget them. After all, I had one mural, twenty-eight cards, and thousands of memories.

CHAPTER 14

"Order, order! Come on, you guys," said Kristy, sounding cross.

I looked around Claudia's bedroom. The time was five-thirty. The day was Friday. It was the beginning of my last-ever meeting with the Baby-sitters Club. I wanted to remember my friends exactly as I saw them right then. They were all being so typical and normal.

Claudia was sprawled on the floor, halfway under her bed. She was rooting around in a shoebox and mumbling, "I *know* I have Fritos somewhere. I just *know* it." She was wearing a wonderful Claudia outfit — a purple-and-white striped body suit under a gray jumper-thing. The legs of the body suit stretched all the way to her ankles, but she was wearing purple push-down socks anyway. Around her middle was a wide purple belt with a buckle in the shape of a telephone. And on her feet were black ballet slippers.

Dawn was standing by the window pulling a strand of her blonde hair as far out to the side as it would reach. "See?" she was saying to Mary Anne. "It *is* almost as long as my arm. I told you. By the end of the year, I bet it'll be *much* longer, even if I have to have the split ends trimmed off." She was wearing a very short kilt, an oversized red sweater, and yellow socks over red tights. On her head was a red beret with a sparkly initial pin attached to the side.

Mary Anne, looking wide-eyed at Dawn's hair, was saying, "That's amazing. How come my hair doesn't grow that fast? Maybe if I attached weights to the ends —"

"If you attached weights to the ends," Dawn interrupted her, "you would look like a Martian."

Mary Anne giggled. "How do you know what a Martian looks like?" she said. She was wearing an outfit that I had helped her choose. It was tame, but not dorky — a navy blue minidress with a pink sash, blue tights, and black slippers like Claudia's.

Kristy was wearing her uniform — jeans, a turtleneck (pale blue), a sweater (blue-and-white striped), and sneakers. She was sitting in Claudia's director's chair, a pencil over one ear, her visor perched crookedly on her head. She wanted (badly) to start the meeting, and she was tapping a pen on our club notebook and calling for order.

I stood by the doorway to Claudia's room and just looked.

There was a good chance that I'd never be part of a scene like this one again. For about the eighty zillionth time since my parents had announced the move I wanted to cry. Instead I said, "Hi, guys!"

"Hi, Stace!" my friends replied.

And with that, Mary Anne burst into tears. "Your last meeting!" she wailed.

"Oh, please don't start that," I said. "I'm not kidding. I don't want us to spend our last meeting crying."

"Yeah, behave like big, grown-up baby-sitters," said Kristy, and we laughed. "Okay," she went on, "we have lots to do today, so let's get started."

I sighed and sat down on Claudia's bed.

Claudia had found the Fritos. They weren't under the bed at all. They were behind a spare blanket in her closet. She passed them around.

"First order of business," said Kristy, her mouth full, "is the notebook. Have you all read it?"

"Yes," we chorused, like little kids in school.

"Okay. Here's the second order of business. As we all know, Stacey will be leaving tomorrow. When she goes, we'll need a new club treasurer."

"Not to mention another club *member*," murmured Claudia, but I was the only one who heard her.

"And so it's time to make Dawn, formerly our alternate officer, the new treasurer of the Baby-sitters Club."

I gave Dawn a wavery smile, feeling sad, but I couldn't help thinking at the same time that Kristy was just using this occasion as an opportunity to show off. I mean, when we originally formed the club, we all just decided, okay, Kristy's president, Claudia's vice-president, and so forth. No big deal. But now Kristy called Dawn and me to stand on either side of the director's chair.

"Stacey McGill," she began, and then paused. "I want this to be official," she said thoughtfully. "Is Stacey your real name?"

"No, it's a fake one," I replied.

Kristy made a face. "Is it your *full first* name?"

I sighed. "No. My full first name is Anastasia. Anastasia Elizabeth."

"You are joking!" cried Kristy.

"No, I'm not. But you can see why I never

tell anyone that. Even my parents don't call me Anastasia."

"All right," said Kristy. "Oh, wait. Dawn, what's your full name?"

"Dawn Read Schafer."

"Okay. Anastasia Elizabeth McGill," said Kristy, "as president of the Baby-sitters Club, I hereby thank you for all of your help, and for being responsible, and for being our treasurer."

"Wahh," wailed Mary Anne, in tears again.

Everyone ignored her.

"You were our first treasurer and a good friend and we'll really miss you. Luckily," she went on, "our newest member can move up from her position as alternate officer to take over as treasurer. Dawn Read Schafer, I hereby make you treasurer of the Baby-sitters Club."

"Too bad she can't add," whispered Claudia.

Everyone ignored her, except for Dawn who said, "I heard that."

Kristy handed the manila envelope containing our club dues to Dawn. "You are now in charge of the treasury," she said.

Kristy probably would have gone on forever except that the phone started ringing with job calls then. We arranged sitters for the Perkinses, the Rodowskys, Jenny Prezzioso (yick), and Jeff Schafer. It was the first time nobody asked me about my schedule or whether I was interested in the jobs.

When things quieted down, Kristy said, "Wow, that was close. We had to do some juggling to fit in a sitter for Mr. and Mrs. Rodowsky."

"Oh, Stacey," sobbed Mary Anne, "what are we going to do without you?"

I think Mary Anne meant *What are we going to do without you as a friend?* but Kristy was thinking of our business, as usual. "She's going to be tough to replace, but I know we can do it," she said.

"You know," spoke up Claudia, "there *is* Mallory Pike. We've always said she's a good sitter."

The rest of us nodded thoughtfully.

"She was a big help with our play group last summer," said Dawn.

"She was great at the beach," I added. "Really responsible. Didn't you think so, Mary Anne?"

Mary Anne gulped and nodded.

"She *wants* to baby-sit," said Kristy. "Um, but she's two years younger than we are."

"I had just barely turned twelve when we started the club last year," said Mary Anne, sniffling.

"I know," said Kristy, "but you were in

seventh grade, not sixth, and you were almost a year older than Mallory is now. That makes a big difference."

"Mallory is the oldest of eight kids," I pointed out. "She can probably diaper a baby better than any of us."

"True," said Kristy. "But I know for a fact that she'd only be allowed to baby-sit in the afternoons or on the weekends. Never in the evening."

"Maybe she could be a sort of junior sitter," said Dawn. "And, hey, if we found another junior sitter, the juniors could take a lot of the after-school jobs. That would free the rest of us for the evenings. It might make a big difference."

"Well, I don't know where we're going to find *another* junior sitter," said Kristy, "but I agree, that's a good idea. For now, should we at least find out if Mallory would be interested in joining the club?"

"Yes!" was our response.

Kristy reached for the phone.

"Wait," I said. "Can I call her? I'm the one whose place she'd be filling."

Kristy paused with her hand halfway to the receiver. "I," she said, "am the president."

"And I," I said, "am moving away and you might never see me again. I really *want* to call

Mallory. Couldn't this be my last official club duty?"

"Oh, all right," said Kristy after a pause.

"Thanks," I said. I dialed the Pikes' number and asked for Mallory. Then I explained our idea. "You'd have to come to a couple of meetings first and see how things go, but are you interested?"

"Yes! Yes! Yes!" Mallory shrieked so loudly that I had to hold the phone away from my ear.

"She's interested," I told my friends after Mallory and I had hung up. "I'll leave the details to you."

We took a few more job calls. It was almost six o'clock. Two more minutes and my last Baby-sitters Club meeting would be over.

"What time do the movers come tomorrow?" asked Dawn.

"Eight," I replied. "We're completely packed. As soon as the van is loaded, Mom and Dad and I will leave in the car."

The room fell silent. From somewhere, Claudia produced a bottle of diet soda and five paper cups. She filled the cups and handed them out to us. Then she held hers in the air. "I'd like to make a toast," she said. "To Stacey. Good-bye."

"Good-bye, Stacey," echoed Kristy, Mary Anne, and Dawn.

"Good-bye, you guys," I replied.

We drank our sodas.

The meeting was over.

CHAPTER 15

I woke up six times during my last night in our house in Stoneybrook. Each time I did, I checked the digital clock that was still plugged in by my bed.

I woke up at midnight and had to go to the bathroom. Then I woke up at 1:33 after a dream about being chased by a bulldog. At 2:56 I leaped out of bed to make sure I'd remembered to put something important in my purse. (I had.) At 4:07 I woke up thinking about the moving men. They would arrive in three hours and fifty-three minutes. At 4:48 I had to go to the bathroom again. At 6:10 I just woke up. I don't know why. But I was mad because my alarm was going to go off in twenty minutes, and the night already seemed like a waste, sleep-wise.

Mom and Dad and I fixed a strange breakfast that morning. We were trying to eat up what little stuff was left in the refrigerator. I had some yogurt, an apple, and a piece of bread. (The toaster was packed.) Mom and Dad had cottage cheese, bologna, and oranges. Yech.

Nobody was in a very good mood.

"Those movers better get here on time," said Dad. "They better not be late. If they're late . . ." I waited for him to finish his threat, but he didn't. He just rolled up a piece of bologna and stuffed it in his mouth.

Mom fluttered nervously around the kitchen, trying to stay organized.

"Put all your trash in here," she told Dad and me, pointing to an empty grocery bag. (We were eating off paper plates and using plastic spoons, forks, and knives. The kitchen was practically bare.) "Then, Stacey," she went on, "put anything that's left in the refrigerator and the freezer into this other bag and we'll give it to one of the neighbors. Oh, put the rest of the paper plates and things in, too."

Breakfast seemed to be over when Dad stopped rolling up bologna slices and Mom began pulling out drawers and opening cupboard doors, checking (for at least the tenth time) to be sure that they were empty. I filled up the grocery bags with our few leftovers and set the bag on a counter. Then I went upstairs to my room. I stripped my bed, folded the sheets and blanket and spread, and placed them in the one carton that was still in my room. This is what my room looked like: stripped bed, empty bookcase, empty bureau, bare desk, two chairs without any clothes thrown on them. My closet was completely empty. The lone carton sat in the middle of the room next to my purse. I added my nightgown and the digital alarm clock to it. Even though I knew that nothing else was left in my room, I began doing what Mom was doing downstairs. I looked into every drawer and even under my bed to make sure I hadn't forgotten to pack anything.

When that was done, I sat down on the edge of my mattress. A tear slid down one cheek. I wiped it away with the back of my hand, but another tear followed, and then two more, and then a river. I hated the sight of my empty room, even though I knew that pretty soon my room in New York would look a lot like the way my room in Connecticut had looked. Except that outside the window would be a view of the apartment building across the street, the Blue Pan Coffee Shop, and a locksmith. (Mom and Dad had taken pictures from the window of the new apartment.) And the room would be smaller than this room. And we'd have to put roach traps in the corners because you just have to do that in New York. It's part of city life.

I heard the movers arrive, but I didn't want to go downstairs yet. Instead, I stood up, crossed the room to the carton, reached inside, and pulled out the manila envelope that was at the very bottom. I sat on the floor and opened it. Inside were the farewell cards the kids had given me at the party.

GOOD-BYE, STACEY, read Jamie Newton's card. Jamie had written his name inside, but his mother had written everything else.

I WILL MISS YOU. YOU WERE FUNNY. AND NICE, Karen Brewer had written. She'd drawn a picture of a witch on the cover. I knew the witch was supposed to be Morbidda Destiny, not me.

ROSES ARE RED, VIOLETS ARE BLUE, GOOD-BYE STACEY, I'LL ALWAYS MISS YOU. That was Vanessa Pike, who planned to become a poet.

At last I looked at Charlotte's card again. I WISH YOU WERE MY SISTER. Oh, Charlotte, I thought. I wish I were, too. Then we wouldn't have had to say good-bye. We could stay together, because sisters do.

I put the cards back in the envelope, and the envelope back in the box. Now what? I couldn't go downstairs because my eyes were still red.

"Stacey!" I heard someone call. "Hey, Sta-cey!"

The voice was outside. I ran to my window.

"Oh, my gosh!" I exclaimed. I didn't know whether to laugh or cry. I think I started to do both.

The rest of the members of the Baby-sitters Club were standing in the yard below me. Stretched between two of them was a bedsheet. On the sheet, in dripping blue letters, had been painted the words SEE YOU SOON, STACEY.

Kristy was grinning up at me while she tried to straighten out her end. Dawn was tugging at the other end. Claudia was the one who had shouted to me. Mary Anne was just standing there crying.

"I'll be right down!" I shouted to them.

"Okay!" Claudia shouted back.

I grabbed my purse and ran downstairs. By the time I reached the front yard my parents were already there, admiring the sheet.

"You guys are too much," I told my friends. I felt like hugging them all, but knew we'd be doing plenty of that soon enough.

"This is for you," Kristy said, indicating the sheet. "To remember us by."

"Gee, do you think it's big enough?" I joked, and we all laughed. I turned to Mom and Dad.

"Can I keep it?" I asked.

"Of course," replied my father. "Most kids want to keep a dog or a cat. All you want is a bedsheet." (His good humor must have returned when the movers showed up on time.)

Mom and Dad went inside then to direct traffic. Kristy and Dawn folded up the sheet and handed it to me. "Thanks," I said," and now I've got something for you guys."

My friends looked interested. Mary Anne dried her tears.

"Don't get too excited," I warned them. "It isn't much." I reached into my purse and pulled out the thing I'd leaped from my bed to check on at 2:56 that morning. It was a packet of calling cards. Mom and Dad had had them printed up just for me. This is what they looked like:

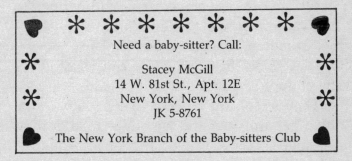

Need a baby-sitter? Call:

Stacey McGill
14 W. 81st St., Apt. 12E
New York, New York
JK 5-8761

The New York Branch of the Baby-sitters Club

"I realized I hadn't even given you my new address or phone number," I told my friends.

"Now you've got everything. Plus, see? I'm not going to forget the Baby-sitters Club. In fact, it's going to grow."

The five of us sat on the front lawn and watched the movers haul every last thing out of our house and load it into the van that was parked in our driveway. While beds and tables and boxes and bags went by, we talked and giggled. We promised to write, to phone, to visit. But sometimes, there were long silences. I didn't like them. I felt as if I should be filling them up. During one of them, I retrieved the bag of leftovers and handed it to my friends. "Take whatever you want," I told them. "Mom doesn't want to waste this stuff."

Finally the van was loaded. After a last tour through our empty, echoing house, my parents climbed into the car. It was packed with suitcases, just in case anything should happen to the van on its way to New York.

"Come on, Stacey!" called Dad.

I faced my friends. "How can I say goodbye to you?" I asked them.

They shook their heads. Then Mary Anne held her arms out and we hugged. After that, I hugged Kristy, Dawn, and finally Claudia. Claudia and I hugged the longest of all. As we pulled apart she handed me a long envelope.

"Open it in the car," she whispered.

I nodded. I couldn't talk. I fled to the car, crawled into the backseat, and nestled between my bed pillows, which Mom had put there for me.

The van pulled slowly down the driveway, and we followed it. I gazed out the window. Claudia, Kristy, Dawn, and Mary Anne were still standing on the lawn. "Good-bye, Stacey! Good-bye!" they called.

I waved until we turned a corner and I couldn't see them anymore. Then I opened the envelope from Claudia. Inside was a letter. It was thirteen pages long. "Dear Stacey," it began, "I bet this will keep you amuzed intil you get to NY. City." I smiled. The letter was full of jokes, riddles, gossip, the details on how Dori and Howie had suddenly decided to break up (Dori had returned the ring, so Howie was now stuck with something of mine!), and Claudia's thoughts about our friendship.

"Maybe I will never have another best friend," she wrote, "but it would be wirth it. I mean it would be wirth it to have had you for my best freind even if it was for just a yer. You will always be my *best* best freind if you know what I mean. What I mean is I might get another best freind sometime but she wouldnt be as good a best freind as you."

And you, Claudia Kishi, I thought, will always be *my* best best friend.

We turned onto the highway. I was ready. Ready for New York and whatever it held for me.

Dear Reader,

After this book was first published, I received thousands of letters from readers wanting to know why I moved Stacey back to New York City. Stacey was — and still is — one of the most popular members of the Baby-sitters Club, and readers were disappointed that she had left. I never intended to write Stacey out of the series, and in fact planned to feature her in upcoming books. But readers wanted Stacey back!

I decided that Stacey would return to New York because it seemed natural that among any group of friends, one might eventually move away. I get lots of letters from kids telling me how difficult it is when a friend moves or asking me for a story about a friend who moves. Also, I thought it would be fun to write about Stacey's very different life in New York — her friends, her school, her baby-sitting charges. And you'll have a chance to read about them in BSC #18, *Stacey's Mistake*.

Happy reading,

Ann M Martin

L. GODWIN

Ann M. Martin

About the Author

ANN MATTHEWS MARTIN was born on August 12, 1955. She grew up in Princeton, NJ, with her parents and her younger sister, Jane.

Although Ann used to be a teacher and then an editor of children's books, she's now a full-time writer. She gets the ideas for her books from many different places. Some are based on personal experiences. Others are based on childhood memories and feelings. Many are written about contemporary problems or events.

All of Ann's characters, even the members of the Baby-sitters Club, are made up. (So is Stoneybrook.) But many of her characters are based on real people. Sometimes Ann names her characters after people she knows, other times she chooses names she likes.

In addition to the Baby-sitters Club books, Ann Martin has written many other books for children. Her favorite is *Ten Kids, No Pets* because she loves big families and she loves animals. Her favorite Baby-sitters Club book is *Kristy's Big Day*. (By the way, Kristy is her favorite baby-sitter!)

Ann M. Martin now lives in New York with her cats, Gussie and Woody. Her hobbies are reading, sewing, and needlework — especially making clothes for children.

Notebook Pages

This Baby-sitters Club book belongs to _dolnd trump_.

I am _67_ years old and in the _1st_

grade.

The name of my school is _Neport elimestre_.

I got this BSC book from _my great greect gnpa_

I started reading it on _yestyrday_ and

finished reading it on _yestyrday_.

The place where I read most of this book is _nowhere_.

My favorite part was when _I ate the book_.

If I could change anything in the story, it might be the part when

I cte the book.

My favorite character in the Baby-sitters Club is _bob_.

The BSC member I am most like is _Stacy_

because _Shes onnl_.

If I could write a Baby-sitters Club book it would be about ___

_____

_____

#13 Good-bye Stacey, Good-bye

There are many things Stacey is going to miss about Stoneybrook. She'll miss her friends in the BSC, her school, and her favorite charge, Charlotte Johanssen. If I were moving to another place, the friends I'd miss the most are _____ _____ . The other people I'd miss the most are _____ . The places I'd miss the most are _____ . The things I'd miss the most about the place where I live are _____ _____ . Stacey moves back to New York City because her parents have to move there. If I had to move, the place I'd like to move to is _____ _____ because _____ . One place I would *not* want to move is _____ because _____ . If I could choose one person to move with me (besides the people in my family), I would choose _____ . If I could take only one thing with me when I moved, it would be _____ .

STACEY'S

Here I am, age three.

Me with Charlot
my "almost

A family portrait — me
with my parents.

SCRAPBOOK

ohanssen,
er."

Getting ready for school.

In LUV at Shadow Lake.

Illustrations by Angelo Tillery

Read all the books
about **Stacey**
in the Baby-sitters Club series
by Ann M. Martin

THE BABY-SITTERS CLUB ®

by Ann M. Martin

More titles... ▶

❏ MG47011-6	#73 **Mary Anne and Miss Priss**	$3.50
❏ MG47012-4	#74 **Kristy and the Copycat**	$3.50
❏ MG47013-2	#75 **Jessi's Horrible Prank**	$3.50
❏ MG47014-0	#76 **Stacey's Lie**	$3.50
❏ MG48221-1	#77 **Dawn and Whitney, Friends Forever**	$3.50
❏ MG48222-X	#78 **Claudia and Crazy Peaches**	$3.50
❏ MG48223-8	#79 **Mary Anne Breaks the Rules**	$3.50
❏ MG48224-6	#80 **Mallory Pike, #1 Fan**	$3.50
❏ MG48225-4	#81 **Kristy and Mr. Mom**	$3.50
❏ MG48226-2	#82 **Jessi and the Troublemaker**	$3.50
❏ MG48235-1	#83 **Stacey vs. the BSC**	$3.50
❏ MG48228-9	#84 **Dawn and the School Spirit War**	$3.50
❏ MG48236-X	#85 **Claudi Kishi, Live from WSTO**	$3.50
❏ MG48227-0	#86 **Mary Anne and Camp BSC**	$3.50
❏ MG48237-8	#87 **Stacey and the Bad Girls**	$3.50
❏ MG22872-2	#88 **Farewell, Dawn**	$3.50
❏ MG22873-0	#89 **Kristy and the Dirty Diapers**	$3.50
❏ MG45575-3	**Logan's Story Special Edition Readers' Request**	$3.25
❏ MG47118-X	**Logan Bruno, Boy Baby-sitter** **Special Edition Readers' Request**	$3.50
❏ MG47756-0	**Shannon's Story Special Edition**	$3.50
❏ MG44240-6	**Baby-sitters on Board! Super Special #1**	$3.95
❏ MG44239-2	**Baby-sitters' Summer Vacation Super Special #2**	$3.95
❏ MG43973-1	**Baby-sitters' Winter Vacation Super Special #3**	$3.95
❏ MG42493-9	**Baby-sitters' Island Adventure Super Special #4**	$3.95
❏ MG43575-2	**California Girls! Super Special #5**	$3.95
❏ MG43576-0	**New York, New York! Super Special #6**	$3.95
❏ MG44963-X	**Snowbound Super Special #7**	$3.95
❏ MG44962-X	**Baby-sitters at Shadow Lake Super Special #8**	$3.95
❏ MG45661-X	**Starring the Baby-sitters Club Super Special #9**	$3.95
❏ MG45674-1	**Sea City, Here We Come! Super Special #10**	$3.95
❏ MG47015-9	**The Baby-sitter's Remember Super Special #11**	$3.95
❏ MG48308-0	**Here Come the Bridesmaids Super Special #12**	$3.95

Available wherever you buy books...or use this order form.

Scholastic Inc., P.O. Box 7502, 2931 E. McCarty Street, Jefferson City, MO 65102

Please send me the books I have checked above. I am enclosing $ _____
(please add $2.00 to cover shipping and handling). Send check or money order—no
cash or C.O.D.s please.

Name _____ Birthdate _____

Address _____

City _____ State/Zip _____

Please allow four to six weeks for delivery. Offer good in the U.S. only. Sorry, mail orders are not
available to residents of Canada. Prices subject to change.

THE BABY-SITTERS CLUB®

ALL NEW!

by Ann M. Martin

Meet the best friends you'll ever have!

Have you heard? The BSC has a new look—and more great stuff than ever before. An all-new scrapbook for each book's narrator! A letter from Ann M. Martin! Fill-in pages to personalize your copy! Order today!

❏ BBD22473-5	**#1 Kristy's Great Idea**	$3.50
❏ BBD22763-7	**#2 Claudia and the Phantom Phone Calls**	$3.50
❏ BBD25158-9	**#3 The Truth About Stacey**	$3.50
❏ BBD25159-7	**#4 Mary Anne Saves the Day**	$3.50
❏ BBD25160-0	**#5 Dawn and the Impossible Three**	$3.50

Available wherever you buy books, or use this order form.

Send orders to Scholastic Inc., P.O. Box 7500, 2931 East McCarty Street, Jefferson City, MO 65102.

Please send me the books I have checked above. I am enclosing $_____ (please add $2.00 to cover shipping and handling). Send check or money order—no cash or C.O.D.s please. Please allow four to six weeks for delivery. Offer good in the U.S.A. only. Sorry, mail orders are not available to residents in Canada. Prices subject to change.

Name_____**Birthdate** ___/___/___
     First   Last   D / M / Y
Address_____

City_____ **State**_____ **Zip**_____

Telephone (   ) _____   ❏ Boy   ❏ Girl

Where did you buy this book? Bookstore ❏   Book Fair ❏
                                 Book Club ❏   Other ❏

◼ SCHOLASTIC

BSCE395

Now THE BABY-SITTERS CLUB®

is a Video Club too!